Charles King

Waring's Peril

Charles King

Waring's Peril

ISBN/EAN: 9783337009182

Printed in Europe, USA, Canada, Australia, Japan

Cover: Foto ©Andreas Hilbeck / pixelio.de

More available books at **www.hansebooks.com**

WARING'S PERIL.

BY

CAPT. CHARLES KING,

U. S. ARMY,

AUTHOR OF "THE COLONEL'S DAUGHTER," "FOES IN AMBUSH," "AN ARMY
PORTIA," "TWO SOLDIERS," "A SOLDIER'S SECRET," ETC.

PHILADELPHIA:
J. B. LIPPINCOTT COMPANY.
1896.

WARING'S PERIL.

BY

CAPT. CHARLES KING,

U. S. ARMY,

AUTHOR OF "THE COLONEL'S DAUGHTER," "FOES IN AMBUSH," "AN ARMY
PORTIA," "TWO SOLDIERS," "A SOLDIER'S SECRET," ETC.

PHILADELPHIA:

J. B. LIPPINCOTT COMPANY.

1896.

WARING'S PERIL.

CHAPTER I.

" ANANĪAS !"

" Ye-as, suh ?"

" What time is it ?"

" Gyahd-mountin' done gone, suh."

" The devil it has ! What do you mean, sir, by allowing me to sleep on in this shameless and unconscionable manner, when an indulgent government is suffering for my services ? What sort of day is it, sir ?"

" Beautiful day, Mr. Waring."

" Then go at once to Mr. Larkin and tell him he can't wear his new silk hat this morning,—I want it, and you fetch it. Don't allow him to ring in the old one on you. Tell him I mean the new 'spring style' he just brought from New York. Tell Mr. Ferry I want that new Hatfield suit of his, and you get Mr. Pierce's silk umbrella; then come back here and get

3

my bath and my coffee. Stop there, Ananias!
Give my pious regards to the commanding
officer, sir, and tell him that there's no drill for
'X' Battery this morning, as I'm to breakfast
at Moreau's at eleven o'clock and go to the
matinée afterwards."

"Beg pahdon, suh, but de cunnle's done
ohdered review fo' de whole command, suh,
right at nine o'clock."

"So much the better. Then Captain Cram
must stay, and won't need his swell team. Go
right down to the stable and tell Jeffers I'll
drive at nine-thirty."

"But——"

"No buts, you incorrigible rascal! I don't
pay you a princely salary to raise obstacles. I
don't pay you at all, sir, except at rare intervals
and in moments of mental decrepitude. Go at
once! Allez! Chassez! Skoot!"

"But, lieutenant," says Ananias, his black
face shining, his even white teeth all agleam,
"Captain Cram stopped in on de way back
from stables to say Glenco 'd sprained his foot
and you was to ride de bay colt. *Please* get
up, suh. Boots and Saddles 'll soun' in ten
minutes."

"It won't, but if it does I'll brain the bugler. Tell him so. Tell Captain Cram he's entirely mistaken: I won't ride the bay colt—nor Glenco. I'm going driving, sir, with Captain Cram's own team and road-wagon. Tell *him* so. Going in forty-five minutes by my watch. Where is it, sir?"

"It ain't back from de jeweller's, suh, where you done lef' it day before yist'day; but his boy's hyuh now, suh, wid de bill for las' year. What shall I tell him?"

"Tell him to go to—quarantine. No! Tell him the fever has broken out here again, sir, and not to call until ten o'clock next spring,— next mainspring they put in that watch. Go and get Mr. Merton's watch. Tell him I'll be sure to overstay in town if he doesn't send it, and then I can't take him up and introduce him to those ladies from Louisville to-morrow. Impress that on him, sir, unless he's gone and left it on his bureau, in which case impress the watch,—the watch, sir, in any case. No! Stop again, Ananias; *not* in any case, only in the gold hunting-case; no other. Now then, vanish!"

"But, lieutenant, 'fo' Gawd, suh, dey'll put you in arrest if you cuts drill dis time. Cunnle

Braxton says to Captain Cram only two days ago, suh, dat——"

But here a white arm shot out from a canopy of mosquito-netting, and first a boot-jack, then a slipper, then a heavy top-boot, came whizzing past the darky's dodging head, and, finding expostulation vain, that faithful servitor bolted out in search of some ally more potent, and found one, though not the one he sought or desired, just entering the adjoining room.

A big fellow, too,—too big, in fact, to be seen wearing, as was the fashion in the sixties, the shell jacket of the light artillery. He had a full round body, and a full round ruddy face, and a little round visorless cap cocked on one side of a round bullet head, not very full of brains, perhaps, yet reputed to be fairly stocked with what is termed "horse sense." His bulky legs were thrust deep in long boots, and ornamented, so far as the skin-tight breeches of sky-blue were concerned, with a scarlet welt along the seam, a welt that his comrades were wont to say would make a white mark on his nose, so red and bulbous was that organ. He came noisily in from the broad veranda overlooking the parade-ground, glanced about on the disarray of the bachelor sitting-room, then whirled on Ananias.

"Mr. Waring dressed?"

"No-o, suh; jus' woke up, suh; ain't out o' bed yit."

"The lazy vagabone! Just let me get at him a minute," said the big man, tramping over to the door-way as though bent on invading the chamber beyond. But Ananias had halted short at sight of the intruder, and stood there resolutely barring the way.

"Beg pahdon, lieutenant, but Mr. Waring ain't had his bath yit. Can I mix de lieutenant a cocktail, suh?"

"Can you? You black imp of Satan, why isn't it ready now, sir? Sure you could have seen I was as dhry as a lime-kiln from the time I came through the gate. Hware's the demijohn, you villain?"

"Bein' refilled, suh, down to de sto', but dar's a little on de sideboa'd, suh," answered Ananias, edging over thither now that he had lured the invader away from the guarded door-way. "Take it straight, suh, o' wid bitters—o' toddy?"

"Faith, I'll answer ye as Pat did the parson:

I'll take it straight now, and then be drinkin' the toddy while your honor is mixin' the punch. Give me hold of it, you smudge! and tell your masther it's review,—full dress,—and it's time for him to be up. Has he had his two cocktails yet?"

"The lieutenant doesn't care fo' any dis mawnin', suh. I'll fetch him his coffee in a minute. Did you see de cunnle's oade'ly, suh? He was lookin' fo' you a moment ago."

The big red man was gulping down a big drink of the fiery liquor at the instant. He set the glass back on the sideboard with unsteady hand and glared at Ananias suspiciously.

"Is it troot' you're tellin', nigger? Hwat did he say was wanted?"

"Didn't say, suh, but de cunnle's in his office. Yawnduh comes de oade'ly, too, suh; guess he must have hyuhd you was over hyuh."

The result of this announcement was not unexpected. The big man made a leap for the chamber door, only to find it slammed in his face from the other side.

"Hwat the devil's the matter with your master this morning, Ananias?—Waring! Waring, I say! Let me in: the K. O.'s orderly

is afther me, and all on account of your bringing me in at that hour last night.—Tell him I've
gone, Ananias.—Let me in, Waring, there's a
good fellow."

"Go to blazes, Doyle!" is the unfeeling answer from the other side. "I'm bathing."
And a vigorous splashing follows the announcement.

"For the Lord's sake, Waring, let me in.
Sure I can't see the colonel now. If I could
stand him off until review and inspection's over
and he's had his dhrink, he'd let the whole
thing drop; but that blackguard of a sinthry
has given us away. Sure I told you he would."

"Then slide down the lightning-rod! Fly
up the chimney! Evaporate! Dry up and blow
away, but get *out!* You can't come in here."

"Oh, for mercy's sake, Waring! Sure 'twas
you that got me into the scrape. You know
that I was dhrunk when you found me up the
levee. You made me come down when I didn't
want to. Hwat did I say to the man last night,
anyhow?"

"Say to him? Poor devil! why, you never
can remember after you're drunk what you've
been doing the night before. Some time it'll

be the death of you. You abused him like
a pickpocket,—the sergeant of the guard and
everybody connected with it."

"Oh, murther, murther, murther!" groaned
the poor Irishman, sitting down and covering
his face with his hands. "Sure they'll court-
martial me this time without fail, and I know it.
For God's sake, Waring, can't ye let a fellow in
and say that I'm not here?"

"Hyuh, dis way, lieutenant," whispered Ananias, mysteriously. "Slip out on de po'ch and
into Mr. Pierce's room. I'll tell you when he's
gone." And in a moment the huge bulk of the
senior lieutenant of Light Battery "X" was
being boosted through a window opening from
the gallery into the bachelor den of the junior
second lieutenant. No sooner was this done
than the negro servant darted back, closed and
bolted the long green Venetian blinds behind
him, tiptoed to the bedroom door, and, softly
tapping, called,—

"Mr. Waring! Mr. Waring! get dressed
quick as you can, suh; I'll lay out your uniform
in hyuh."

"I tell you, Ananias, I'm going to town, sir;
not to any ridiculous review. Go and get what

I ordered you. See that I'm properly dressed, sir, or I'll discharge you. Confound you, sir! there isn't a drop of Florida water in this bath, and none on my bureau. Go and rob Mr. Pierce,—or anybody."

But Ananias was already gone. Darting out on the gallery, he took a header through the window of the adjoining quarters through which Mr. Doyle had escaped, snatched a long flask from the dressing-table, and was back in the twinkling of an eye.

"What became of Mr. Doyle?" asked Waring, as he thrust a bare arm through a narrow aperture to receive the spoil. "Don't let him get drunk; *he's* got to go to review, sir. If he doesn't, Colonel Braxton may be so inconsiderate as to inquire why both the lieutenants of 'X' Battery are missing. Take good care of him till the review, sir, then let him go to grass; and don't you dare leave me without Florida water again, if you have to burglarize the whole post. What's Mr. Doyle doing, sir?"

"Peekin' froo de blin's in Mr. Pierce's room, suh; lookin' fo' de oade'ly. I done told him de cunnle was ahter him, but he ain't, suh," chuckled Ananias. "I fixed it all right wid de

gyahd dis mawnin', suh. Dey won' tell 'bout
his cuttin' up las' night. He'd forgot de whole
t'ing, suh; he allays does; he never does know
what's happened de night befo'. He wouldn't
'a' known about dis, but I told his boy Jim to
tell him 'bout it ahter stables. I told Jim to
sweah dat dey'd repohted it to de cunnle."

"Very well, Ananias; very well, sir; you're
a credit to your name. Now go and carry out
my orders. Don't forget Captain Cram's wagon.
Tell Jeffers to be here with it on time." And
the lieutenant returned to his bath without waiting for reply.

"Ye-as, suh," was the subordinate answer, as
Ananias promptly turned, and, whistling cheer-
ily, went banging out upon the gallery and
clattering down the open stairway to the brick-
paved court below. Here he as promptly
turned, and, noiseless as a cat, shot up the stair-
way, tiptoed back into the sitting-room, kicked
off his low-heeled slippers, and rapidly, but
with hardly an audible sound, resumed the
work on which he had been engaged,—the
arrangement of his master's kit.

Already, faultlessly brushed, folded and hanging over the back of a chair close by the cham-

ber door were the bright blue, scarlet-welted
battery trousers then in vogue, very snug at the
knee, very springy over the foot. Underneath
them, spread over the square back of the chair,
a dark-blue, single-breasted frock-coat, hanging
nearly to the floor, its shoulders decked with
huge epaulettes, to the right one of which were
attached the braid and loops of a heavy gilt
aiguillette whose glistening pendants were hung
temporarily on the upper button. On the seat
of the chair was folded a broad soft sash of red
silk net, its tassels carefully spread. Beside it
lay a pair of long buff gauntlets, new and spotless. At the door, brilliantly polished, stood a
pair of buttoned gaiter boots, the heels deco-
rated with small glistening brass spurs. In the
corner, close at hand, leaned a long curved
sabre, its gold sword-knot, its triple-guarded
hilt, its steel scabbard and plated bands and
rings, as well as the swivels and buckle of the
black sword-belt, showing the perfection of finish in manufacture and care in keeping. From a
round leather box Ananias now extracted a new
gold-wire *fouragère,* which he softly wiped with
a silk handkerchief, dandled lovingly an instant
the glistening tassels, coiled it carefully upon

2

the sash, then producing from the same box a
long scarlet horsehair plume he first brushed it
into shimmering freedom from the faintest knot
or kink, then set it firmly through its socket into
the front of a gold-braided shako whose black
front was decked with the embroidered cross
cannon of the regiment, surmounted by the
arms of the United States. This he noiselessly
placed upon the edge of the mantel, stepped
back to complacently view his work, flicked off
a possible speck of dust on the sleeve of the
coat, touched with a chamois-skin the gold crescent of the nearest epaulette, then softly, noiselessly as before vanished through the door-way,
tiptoed to the adjoining window, and peeked in.
Mr. Doyle had thrown himself into Pierce's
arm-chair, and was trying to read the morning
paper.

"Wunner what Mars'er Pierce will say when
he gits back from breakfast," was Ananias's
comment, as he sped softly down the stairs, a
broad grin on his black face, a grin that almost
instantly gave place to preternatural solemnity
and respect as, turning sharply on the sidewalk
at the foot of the stairs, he came face to face
with the battery commander. Ananias would

have passed with a low obeisance, but the captain halted him short.

"Where's Mr. Waring, sir?"

"Dressin' fo' inspection, captain."

"He is? I just heard in the mess-room that he didn't propose attending,—that he had an engagement to breakfast and was going in town."

"Ye-as, suh, ye-as, suh, General Roosseau, suh, expected de lieutenant in to breakfast, but de moment he hyuhd 'twas review he ohdered me to git everything ready, suh. I's goin' for de bay colt now. Beg pahdon, captain, de lieutenant says is de captain goin' to wear gauntlets or gloves dis mawnin'? He wants to do just as de captain does, suh."

What a merciful interposition of divine Providence it is that the African cannot blush! Captain Cram looked suspiciously at the earnest, unwinking, black face before him. Some memory of old college days flitted through his mind at the moment. "O Kunopes!" ("thou dog-faced one!") he caught himself muttering, but negro diplomacy was too much for him, and the innocence in the face of Ananias would have baffled a man far more suspicious. Cram was

a fellow who loved his battery and his profession as few men loved before. He was full of
big ideas in one way and little oddities in
another. Undoubted ability had been at the
bottom of his selection over the head of many
a senior to command one of the light batteries
when the general dismounting took place in '66.
Unusual attractions of person had won him a
wife with a fortune only a little later. The
fortune had warranted a short leave abroad this
very year. (He would not have taken a day
over sixty, for fear of losing his light battery.)
He had been a stickler for gauntlets on all
mounted duty when he went away, and he came
home converted to white wash-leather gloves
because the British horse-artillery wore no
other, "and they, sir, are the nattiest in the
world." He could not tolerate an officer whose
soul was not aflame with enthusiasm for battery
duty, and so was perpetually at war with Waring, who dared to have other aspirations. He
delighted in a man who took pride in his dress
and equipment, and so rejoiced in Waring, who,
more than any subaltern ever attached to "X,"
was the very glass of soldier fashion and mould
of soldier form. He had dropped in at the

bachelor mess just in time to hear some gab-
bling youngster blurt out a bet that Sam Waring would cut review and keep his tryst in
town, and he had known him many a time to
overpersuade his superiors into excusing him
from duty on pretext of social claims, and more
than once into pardoning deliberate absence.
But he and the post commander had deemed it
high time to block all that nonsense in future,
and had so informed him, and were nonplussed
at Waring's cheery acceptance of the implied
rebuke and most airy, graceful, and immediate
change of the subject. The whole garrison was
chuckling over it by night.

"Why, certainly, colonel," said he, "I *have*
been most derelict of late during the visit of
all these charming people from the North; and
that reminds me, some of them are going to
drive out here to hear the band this afternoon
and take a bite at my quarters. I was just on
my way to beg Mrs. Braxton and Mrs. Cram to
receive for me, when your orderly came. And,
colonel, I want your advice about the champagne. Of course I needn't say I hope you
both will honor me with your presence." Old
Brax loved champagne and salad better than

b   2*

anything his profession afforded, and was disarmed at once. As for Cram, what could he say when the post commander dropped the matter? With all his daring disregard of orders and established customs, with all his consummate *sang-froid* and what some called impudence and others "check," every superior under whom he had ever served had sooner or later become actually fond of Sam Waring,— even stern old Rounds,—"old Double Rounds" the boys called him, one of the martinets of the service, whose first experience with the fellow was as memorable as it was unexpected, and who wound up, after a vehement scoring of some two minutes' duration, during which Waring had stood patiently at attention with an expression of the liveliest sympathy and interest on his handsome face, by asking impressively, "Now, sir, what have you to say for yourself?"

To which, with inimitable mixture of suavity and concern, Sam replied, "Nothing whatever, sir. I doubt if anything more could be said. I had no adequate idea of the extent of my misdoing. Have I your permission to sit down, sir, and think it over?"

Rounds actually didn't know what to think,

and still less what to say. Had he believed for
an instant that the young gentleman was insin-
cere, he would have had him in close arrest in
the twinkling of an eye; but Waring's tone and
words and manner were those of contrition
itself. It was not possible that one of the boys
should dare to be guying him, the implacable
Rounds, "old Grand Rounds" of the Sixth
Corps, old Double Rounds of the horse-artillery
of the Peninsula days. Mrs. Rounds had her
suspicions when told of the affair, but was silent,
for of all the officers stationed in and around
the old Southern city Sam Waring was by long
odds the most graceful and accomplished dancer
and german leader, the best informed on all
manner of interesting matters,—social, musical,
dramatic, fashionable,—the prime mover in garrison hops and parties, the connecting link
between the families of the general and staff
officers in town and the linesmen at the sur-
rounding posts, the man whose dictum as to a
dinner or luncheon and whose judgment as to a
woman's toilet were most quoted and least questioned, the man whose word could almost make
or mar an army girl's success; and good old
Lady Rounds had two such encumbrances the

first winter of their sojourn in the South, and
two army girls among so many are subjects of
not a little thought and care. If Mr. Waring
had not led the second german with Margaret
Rounds the mother's heart would have been
well-nigh crushed. It was fear of some such
catastrophe that kept her silent on the score of
Waring's reply to her irate lord, for if Sam did
mean to be impertinent, as he unquestionably
could be, the colonel she knew would be merci-
less in his discipline and social amenities would
be at instant end. Waring had covered her
with maternal triumph and Margaret with
bliss unutterable by leading the ante-Lenten
german with the elder daughter and making
her brief stay a month of infinite joy. The
Rounds were ordered on to Texas, and Margaret's brief romance was speedily and properly
forgotten in the devotions of a more solid if less
fascinating fellow. To do Waring justice, he
had paid the girl no more marked attention
than he showed to any one else. He would
have led the next german with Genevieve had
there been another to lead, just as he had led
previous affairs with other dames and damsels.
It was one of the ninety-nine articles of his

social faith that a girl should have a good time her first season, just as it was another that a bride should have a lovely wedding, a belle at least one offer a month, a married woman as much attention at an army ball as could be lavished on a bud. He prided himself on the fact that no woman at the army parties given that winter had remained a wall-flower. Among such a host of officers as was there assembled during the year that followed on the heels of the war it was no difficult matter, to be sure, to find partners for the thirty or forty ladies who honored those occasions with their presence. Of local belles there were none. It was far too soon after the bitter strife to hope for bliss so great as that. There were hardly any but army women to provide for, and even the bulkiest and least attractive of the lot was led out for the dance. Waring would go to any length to see them on the floor but that of being himself the partner. There the line was drawn irrevocably. The best dancer among the men, he simply would not dance except with the best dancers among the women. As to personal appearance and traits, it may be said first that Waring was a man of slender, graceful phy-

sique, with singularly well shaped hands and
feet and a head and face that were almost too
good-looking to be manly. Dark hazel eyes,
dark brown hair, eyebrows, lashes, and a very
heavy drooping moustache, a straight nose, a
soft, sensitive mouth with even white teeth that
were, however, rarely visible, a clear-cut chin,
and with it all a soft, almost languid Southern
intonation, musical, even ultra-refined, and he
shrank like a woman from a coarse word or the
utterance of an impure thought. He was a man
whom many women admired, of whom some
were afraid, whom many liked and trusted, for
he could not be bribed to say a mean thing
about one of their number, though he would
sometimes be satirical to her very face. It was
among the men that Sam Waring was hated
or loved,—loved, laughed over, indulged, even
spoiled, perhaps, to any and every extent, by
the chosen few who were his chums and intimates, and absolutely hated by a very considerable element that was prominent in the army in
those queer old days,—the array of officers who,
by reason of birth, antecedents, lack of education or of social opportunities, were wanting in
those graces of manner and language to which

Waring had been accustomed from earliest boyhood. His people were Southerners, yet, not
being slave-owners, had stood firm for the
Union, and were exiled from the old home as
a natural consequence in a war in which the
South held all against who were not for her.
Appointed a cadet and sent to the Military
Academy in recognition of the loyalty of his
immediate relatives, he was not graduated until
the war was practically over, and then, gazetted
to an infantry regiment, he was stationed for a
time among the scenes of his boyhood, ostra-
cized by his former friends and unable to asso-
ciate with most of the war-worn officers among
whom his lot was cast. It was a year of misery,
that ended in long and dangerous illness, his
final shipment to Washington on sick-leave, and
then a winter of keen delight, a social campaign
in which he won fame, honors, friends at court,
and a transfer to the artillery, and then, joining
his new regiment, he plunged with eagerness
into the gayeties of city life. The blues were
left behind with the cold facings of his former
corps, and hope, life, duty, were all blended in
hues as roseate as his new straps were red. It
wasn't a month before all the best fellows in the

batteries swore by Sam Waring and all the others at him, so that where there were five who liked there were at least twenty who didn't, and these made up in quantity what they lacked in quality.

To sum up the situation, Lieutenant Doyle's expression was perhaps the most comprehensive, as giving the views of the great majority: "If I were his K. O. and this crowd the coort, he'd 'a' been kicked out of the service months ago."

And yet, entertaining or expressing so hostile an opinion of the laughing lieutenant, Mr. Doyle did not hesitate to seek his society on many an occasion when he wasn't wanted, and to solace himself at Waring's sideboard at any hour of the day or night, for Waring kept what was known as "open house" to all comers, and the very men who wondered how he could afford it and who predicted his speedy swamping in a mire of debt and disgrace were the very ones who were most frequently to be found loafing about his gallery, smoking his tobacco and swigging his whiskey, a pretty sure sign that the occupant of the quarters, however, was absent. With none of their number had he ever had open quarrel. Remarks made at his expense and reported to him in moments of bibulous confidence he treated with gay disdain, often to the manifest disappointment of his informant. In his presence even the most reckless of their number were conscious of a certain restraint. Waring, as has been said, detested foul language, and had a very quiet but effective way of suppressing it, often without so much as uttering a word. These were the rough days of the army, the very roughest it ever knew, the days that intervened between the incessant strain and tension of the four years' battling and the slow gradual resumption of good order and military discipline. The rude speech and manners of the camp still permeated every garrison. The bulk of the commissioned force was made up of hard fighters, brave soldiers and loyal servants of the nation, to be sure, but as a class they had known no other life or language since the day of their muster-in. Of the line officers stationed in and around this Southern city in the lovely spring-tide of 186–, of a force aggregating twenty companies of infantry and cavalry, there were fifty captains and lieutenants appointed from the volunteers, the ranks, or civil life, to one graduated from

West Point. The predominance was in favor
of ex-sergeants, corporals, or company clerks,
—good men and true when they wore the
chevrons, but who, with a few marked and
most admirable exceptions, proved to be utterly
out of their element when promoted to a higher
sphere. The entrance into their midst of Captain Cram with his swell light battery, with
officers and men in scarlet plumes and full-
dress uniforms, was a revelation to the sombre
battalions whose officers had not yet even pur-
chased their epaulettes and had seen no occasion
to wear them. But when Cram and his lieutenants came swaggering about the garrison
croquet-ground in natty shell jackets, Russian
shoulder-knots, riding-breeches, boots, and spurs,
there were not lacking those among the sturdy
foot who looked upon the whole proceeding
with great disfavor. Cram had two "rankers"
with him when he came, but one had trans-
ferred out in favor of Waring, and now his
battery was supplied with the full complement
of subalterns,—Doyle, very much out of place,
commanding the right section (as a platoon was
called in those days), Waring commanding the
left, Ferry serving as chief of caissons, and

Pierce as battery adjutant and general utility man. Two of the officers were graduates of West Point and not yet three years out of the cadet uniform. Under these circumstances it was injudicious in Cram to sport in person the aiguillettes and thereby set an example to his subalterns which they were not slow to follow. With their gold hat-braids, cords, tassels, and epaulettes, with scarlet plumes and facings, he and his officers were already much more gorgeously bedecked than were their infantry friends. The post commander, old Rounds, had said nothing, because he had had his start in the light artillery and might have lived and died a captain had he not pushed for a volunteer regiment and fought his way up to a division command and a lieutenant-colonelcy of regulars at the close of the war, while his seniors who stuck to their own corps never rose beyond the possibilities of their arm of the service and probably never will. But Braxton, who succeeded as post commander, knew that in European armies and in the old Mexican War days the aiguillette was ordinarily the distinctive badge of general officers or those empowered to give orders in their name. It wasn't the proper thing for a linesman—battery, cavalry, or foot—to wear, said Brax, and he thought Cram was wrong in wearing it, even though some other battery officers did so. But Cram was just back from Britain.

"Why, sir, look at the Life Guards! Look at the Horse Guards in London! Every officer and man wears the aiguillette." And Braxton was a Briton by birth and breeding, and that ended it,—at least so nearly ended it that Cram's diplomatic invitation to come up and try some Veuve Clicquot, extra dry, upon the merits of which he desired the colonel's opinion, had settled it for good and all. Braxton's officers who ventured to suggest that he trim the plumage of these popinjays only got snubbed, therefore, for the time being, and ordered to buy the infantry full dress forthwith, and Cram and his quartette continued to blaze forth in gilded panoply until long after Sam Waring led his last german within those echoing walls and his name lived only as a dim and mist-wreathed memory in the annals of old Jackson Barracks.

But on this exquisite April morning no fellow in all the garrison was more prominent, if not more popular. Despite the slight jealousy existing between the rival arms of the service, there were good fellows and gallant men among the infantry officers at the post, who were as cordially disposed towards the gay lieutenant as were the comrades of his own (colored) cloth. This is the more remarkable because he was never known to make the faintest effort to conciliate anybody and was utterly indifferent to public opinion. It would have been fortune far better than his deserts, but for the fact that by nature he was most generous, courteous, and considerate. The soldiers of the battery were devoted to him. The servants, black or white, would run at any time to do his capricious will. The garrison children adored him. There was simply no subject under discussion at the barracks in those days on which such utter variety of opinion existed as the real character of Lieutenant Sam Waring. As to his habits there was none whatever. He was a *bon vivant*, a "swell," a lover of all that was sweet and fair and good and gracious in life. Self-indulgent, said everybody; selfish, said some; lazy, said many, who watched him day-dreaming through the haze of cigar-smoke until a drive, a hop, a

3*

ride, or an opera-party would call him into
action. Slow, said the men, until they saw him
catch Mrs. Winslow's runaway horse just at
that ugly turn in the levee below the south
tower. Cold-hearted, said many of the women,
until Baby Brainard's fatal illness, when he
watched by the little sufferer's side and brought
her flowers and luscious fruit from town, and
would sit at her mother's piano and play soft,
sweet melodies and sing in low tremulous tone
until the wearied eyelids closed and the sleep no
potion could bring to that fever-racked brain
would come at last for him to whom child-love
was incense and music at once a passion and a
prayer. Men who little knew and less liked
him thought his enmity would be but light, and
few men knew him so well as to realize that his
friendship could be firm and true as steel.

And so the garrison was mixed in its mind as
to Mr. Waring, and among those who heard it
said at the mess that he meant at all hazards to
keep his engagement to breakfast in town there
were some who really wished he might cut
the suddenly-ordered review and thereby bring
down upon his shapely, nonchalant head the
wrath of Colonel Braxton.

"Boots and Saddles" had sounded at the artillery barracks. Mr. Pierce, as battery officer of the day, had clattered off through the north gateway. The battery had marched with dancing plumes and clanking sabres out to the stables and gun-shed. The horses of Lieutenants Doyle and Ferry were waiting for their riders underneath the gallery of their quarters. Captain Cram, in much state, followed by his orderly bugler and guidon-bearer, all in full uniform, was riding slowly down the sunny side of the garrison, and at sight of him Doyle and Ferry, who were leisurely pulling on their gauntlets in front of their respective doors, hooked up their sabres and came clattering down their stairway; but no Waring had appeared. There, across the parade on the southern side, the bay colt, caparisoned in Waring's unimpeachable horse-equipments, was being led up and down in the shade of the quarters, Mr. Pierce's boy Jim officiating as groom, while his confrère Ananias, out of sight, was at the moment on his knees fastening the strap of his master's riding-trousers underneath the dainty gaiter boot, Mr. Waring the while surveying the proceeding over the rim of his coffee-cup.

"Dar, suh. Now into de coat, quick! Yawn-duh goes Captain Cram."

"Ananias, how often have I told you that, howsoever necessary it might be for you to hurry, I never do? It's unbecoming an officer and a gentleman to hurry, sir."

"But you's got to inspect yo' section, suh, befo' you can repote to Captain Cram. Please hurry wid de sash, suh." And, holding the belt extended with both hands, Ananias stood eager to clasp it around Waring's slender waist, but the lieutenant waved him away.

"Get thee behind me, imp of Satan! Would you have me neglect one of the foremost articles of an artilleryman's faith? Never, sir! If there were a wrinkle in that sash it would cut a chasm in my reputation, sir." And, so saying, he stepped to the open door-way, threw the heavy tassel over and around the knob, kissed his hand jauntily to his battery commander, now riding down the opposite side of the parade, backed deliberately away the full length of the sash across the room, then, humming a favorite snatch from "Faust," deliberately wound himself into the bright crimson web, and, making a broad flat loop near the

farther end and without stopping his song,
nodded coolly to Ananias to come on with the
belt. In the same calm and deliberate fashion
he finished his military toilet, set his shako well
forward on his forehead, the chin-strap hanging just below the under lip, 'pulled on the
buff gauntlets, surveyed himself critically and
leisurely in the glass, and then began slowly to
descend the stairs.

"Wait—jus' one moment, please, suh," implored Ananias, hastening after him. "Jus'
happened to think of it, suh: Captain Cram's
wearin' gloves dis mawnin'."

"Ah! So much the more chance to come
back here in ten minutes.—Whoa, coltikins:
how are you this morning, sir? Think you
could run away if I begged you to pretty hard?
You'll try, won't you, old boy?" said Waring,
stroking the glossy neck of the impatient bay.—
"Now, Jim, let go. Never allow anybody to
hold a horse for you when you mount. That's
highly unprofessional, sir. That'll do." And,
so saying, he swung himself into saddle, and,
checking the bounds of his excited colt, rode
calmly away to join the battery.

Already the bandsmen were marching through

c

the north gate on the way to the broad open field in which the manœuvres were held. The adjutant, sergeant-major, and markers were following. Just outside the gate the post commander was seated on horseback, and Cram had reined in to speak with him. Now, in his blithest, cheeriest tones, Waring accosted them, raising his hand in salute as he did so:

"Good-morning, colonel. Good-morning, Captain Cram. We're in luck to-day. Couldn't possibly have lovelier weather. I'm only sorry this came off so suddenly and I hadn't time to invite our friends out from town. They would have been so pleased to see the battalion,—the ceremonies."

"H'm! There was plenty of time if you'd returned to the post at retreat yesterday, sir," growled old Braxton. "Everybody was notified who was here then. What time *did* you get back, sir?"

"Upon my word, colonel, I don't know. I never thought to look or inquire; but it was long after taps. Pardon me, though, I see I'm late inspecting." And in a moment he was riding quietly around among his teams and guns, narrowly scrutinizing each toggle, trace, and strap before taking station midway between his lead drivers, and then, as Cram approached, reporting, "Left section ready, sir."

Meantime, the infantry companies were marching out through the gate and then ordering arms and resting until adjutant's call should sound. Drivers and cannoneers were dismounted to await the formation of the battalion line. Waring rode forward and in the most jovial offhand way began telling Cram of the incidents of the previous day and his sight-seeing with the party of visitors from the North.

"By the way, I promised Mr. Allerton that they should see that team of yours before they left: so, if you've no objection, the first morning you're on duty and can't go up, I'll take advantage of your invitation and drive Miss Allerton myself. Doesn't that court adjourn this week?"

"I'm afraid not," said Cram, grimly. "It looks as though we'd have to sit to-day and to-morrow both."

"Well, that's too bad! They all want to meet you again. Couldn't you come up this evening after stables? Hello! this won't do; our infantry friends will be criticising us: I see you're wearing gloves, and I'm in gauntlets. So is Doyle. We can't fit him out, I'm afraid, but I've just got some from New York exactly like yours. I'll trot back while we're waiting, if you don't object, and change them."

Cram didn't want to say yes, yet didn't like to say no. He hesitated, and—was lost. In another moment, as though never imagining refusal were possible, Waring had quickly ridden away through the gate and disappeared behind the high brick wall.

When the bugle sounded "mount," three minutes later, and the battery broke into column of pieces to march away to the manœuvring grounds, Mr. Ferry left the line of caissons and took command of the rear section. All that the battery saw of Waring or his mount the rest of the morning was just after reaching the line, when the fiery colt came tearing riderless around the field, joyously dodging every attempt of the spectators to catch him, and revelling in the delight of kicking up his heels and showing off in the presence and sight of his envious friends in harness. Plunge though they might, the horses could not join; dodge though they might, the bipeds could not catch him. Review, inspection, and the long ceremonials of the morning went off without the junior first lieutenant of Battery "X," who, for his part, went off without ceremony of any kind, Cram's stylish team and wagon with him. That afternoon he reappeared driving about the barrack square, a pretty girl at his side, both engrossed in the music of the band and apparently oblivious of the bottled-up wrath of either battery or post commander.

"Be gorra!" said Doyle, "I'd like to be in his place now, provided I didn't have to be in it to-morrow."

But when the morrow came there came **no** Waring with it.

CHAPTER II.

For twenty-four hours old Brax had been mad as a hornet. He was not much of a drill-master or tactician, but he thought he was, and it delighted him to put his battalion through the form of review, the commands for which he had memorized thoroughly and delivered with resonant voice and with all proper emphasis. What he did not fancy, and indeed could not do, was the drudge-work of teaching the minutiæ of the school of the battalion, explaining each movement before undertaking its execution. This was a matter he delegated to one of his senior captains. For a week, therefore, in preparation for a possible visit on the part of the new brigadier-general or his inspector, the six companies of the regiment stationed at the post had been fairly well schooled in the cere-monies of review and parade, and so long as nothing more was required of them than a march past in quick time and a ten minutes' stand in line all might go well. The general had unexpectedly appeared one evening with only a single aide-de-camp, simply, as he explained, to return the calls of the officers of the garrison, six or eight of whom had known enough to present themselves and pay their respects in person when he arrived in town. Braxton swelled with gratified pride at the general's praise of the spick-span condition of the parade, the walks, roads, and visible quarters. But it was the very first old-time garrison the new chief had ever seen, a splendid fighting record with the volunteers during the war, and the advantage of taking sides for the Union from a doubtful State, having conspired to win him a star in the regular service only a year or two before.

"We would have had out the battery and given you a salute, sir," said Brax, "had we known you were coming; but it's after retreat now. Next time, general, if you'll ride down some day, I'll be proud to give you a review of the whole command. We have a great big field back here."

And the general had promised to come. This necessitated combined preparation, hence the

order for full-dress rehearsal with battery and
all, and then came confusion. Fresh from the
command of his beautiful horse-battery and the
dashing service with a cavalry division, Cram
hated the idea of limping along, as he expressed
it, behind a battalion of foot, and said so, and
somebody told Brax he had said so,—more than
one somebody, probably, for Brax had many
an adviser to help keep him in trouble. The
order that Cram should appear for instruction
in review of infantry and artillery combined
gave umbrage to the battery commander, and
his reported remarks thereupon, renewed cause
for displeasure to his garrison chief.

"So far as we're concerned," said Cram, who
wanted to utilize the good weather for battery
drill, "we need no instruction, as we have done
the trick time and again before; and if we
hadn't, who in the bloody Fifty-First is there to
teach us? Certainly not old Brax."

All the same the order was obeyed, and Cram
started out that loveliest of lovely spring morn-
ings not entirely innocent of the conviction that
he and his fellows were going to have some
fun out of the thing before they got through
with it. Not that he purposed putting any

hitch or impediment in the way. He meant to do just exactly as he was bid; and so, when adjutant's call had sounded and the blue lines of the infantry were well out on the field, he followed in glittering column of pieces, his satin-coated horses dancing in sheer exuberance of spirits and his red-crested cannoneers sitting with folded arms, erect and statuesque, upon the ammunition-chests. Mrs. Cram, in her pretty basket phaeton, with Mrs. Lawrence, of the infantry, and several of the ladies of the garrison in ambulances or afoot, had taken station well to the front of the forming line. Then it became apparent that old Brax purposed to figure as the reviewing officer and had delegated Major Minor to command the troops. Now, Minor had been on mustering and disbursing duty most of the war, had never figured in a review with artillery before, and knew no more about battery tactics than Cram did of diplomacy. Mounted on a sedate old sorrel, borrowed from the quartermaster for the occasion, with an antiquated, brass-bound Jenifer saddle, minus breast-strap and housings of any kind, but equipped with his better half's brown leather bridle, Minor knew perfectly well he

was only a guy, and felt indignant at Brax for
putting him in so false a plight. He took his
station, however, in front of the regimental
colors, without stopping to think where the
centre of the line might be after the battery
came, and there awaited further developments.
Cram kept nobody waiting, however: his leading team was close at the nimble heels of Captain
Lawrence's company as it marched gayly forth
to the music of the band. He formed sections
at the trot the instant the ground was clear, then
wheeled into line, passed well to the rear of the
prolongation of the infantry rank, and by a
beautiful countermarch came up to the front and
halted exactly at the instant that Lawrence, with
the left flank company, reached his post, each
caisson accurately in trace of its piece, each
team and carriage exactly at its proper interval,
and with his crimson silk guidon on the right
flank and little Pierce signalling "up" or
"back" from a point outside where he could
verify the alignment of the gun-wheels on the
rank of the infantry, Cram was able to command "front" before little Drake, the adjutant,
should have piped out his shrill "Guides posts."

But Drake didn't pipe. There stood all the

companies at support, each captain at the inner flank, and the guides with their inverted muskets still stolidly gazing along the line. It was time for him to pipe, but, instead of so doing, there he stuck at the extreme right, glaring down towards the now immovable battery and its serene commander, and the little adjutant's face was getting redder and puffier every minute.

"Go ahead! What are you waiting for?" hoarsely whispered the senior captain.

"Waiting for the battery to dress," was the stanch reply. Then aloud the shrill voice swept down the line: "Dress that battery to the right!"

Cram looked over a glittering shoulder to the right of the line, where stood the diminutive infantryman. The battery had still its war allowance of horses, three teams to each carriage, lead, swing, and wheel, and that brought its captain far out to the front of the sombre blue rank of foot,—so far out, in fact, that he was about on line with Major Minor, though facing in opposite direction. Perfectly confident that he was exactly where he should be, yet equally determined to abide by any order he might receive, even though he fully understood the cause of Drake's delay, Cram promptly rode

over to the guidon and ordered "Right dress,"
at which every driver's head and eyes were
promptly turned, but not an inch of a wheel,
for the alignment simply could not be improved.
Then after commanding "front" the captain as
deliberately trotted back to his post without so
much as a glance at the irate staff officer. It
was just at this juncture that the bay colt came
tearing down the field, his mane and tail
streaming in the breeze, his reins and stirrups
dangling. In the course of his gyrations about
the battery and the sympathetic plunging of
the teams some slight disarrangement occurred.
But when he presently decided on a rush for
the stables, the captain re-established the alignment as coolly as before, and only noticed as he
resumed his post that the basket phaeton and
Mrs. Cram had gone. Alarmed, possibly, by
the non-appearance of her warm friend Mr.
Waring and the excited gambolings of his
vagrant steed, she had promptly driven back to
the main garrison to see if any accident had
occurred, the colt meantime amusing himself
in a game of fast-and-loose with the stable
guard.

Then it was that old Brax came down and

took a hand. Riding to where Minor still sat on his patient sorrel, the senior bluntly inquired,—

"What the devil's the matter?"

"I don't know," said Minor.

"Who does know?"

"Well, Drake, possibly, or else he doesn't know anything. He's been trying to get Cram to dress his battery back."

"Why, yes, confound it! he's a mile ahead of the line," said the colonel, and off he trotted to expostulate with the batteryman. "Captain Cram, isn't there room for your battery back of the line instead of in front of it?" inquired the chief, in tone both aggrieved and aggressive.

"Lots, sir," answered Cram, cheerfully. "Just countermarched there."

"Then I wish you'd oblige me by moving back at once, sir: you're delaying the whole ceremony here. I'm told Mr. Drake has twice ordered you to dress to the right."

"I've heard it, sir, only once, but have dressed twice, so it's all right," responded Cram, as affably as though he had no other aim in life than to gratify the whims of his post commander.

"Why, confound it, sir, it isn't all right by a

da——good deal! Here you are 'way out on
line with Major Minor, and your battery's——
why, it isn't dressed on our rank at all, sir.
Just look at it."

Cram resumed the carry with the sabre he
had lowered in salute, calmly reversed so as to
face his battery, and, with preternatural gravity
of mien, looked along his front. There midway
between his lead drivers sat Mr. Doyle, his face
well-nigh as red as his plume, his bleary eyes
nearly popping out of his skull in his effort to
repress the emotions excited by this colloquy.
There midway between the lead drivers in the
left section sat Mr. Ferry, gazing straight to
the front over the erected ears of his handsome
bay and doing his very best to keep a solemn
face, though the unshaded corners of his boyish
mouth were twitching with mischief and merriment. There, silent, disciplined, and rigid, sat
the sergeants, drivers, and cannoneers of famous
old Light Battery " X," all agog with interest in
the proceedings and all looking as though they
never heard a word.

"I declare, sir," said Cram, with exasperating
civility, "I can see nothing out of the way.
Will you kindly indicate what is amiss?"

This was too much for Ferry. In his effort
to restrain his merriment and gulp down a
rising flood of laughter there was heard an ex-
plosion that sounded something like the sudden collapse of an inflated paper bag, and old
Brax, glaring angrily at the boy, now red in
the face with mingled mirth and consternation,
caught sudden idea from the sight. Was the
battery laughing at—was the battery commander guying—him? Was it possible that
they were profiting by his ignorance of their
regulations? It put him on his guard and suggested a tentative.

"Do you mean that you are right in being so
far ahead of our line instead of dressed upon it?"
asked he of the big blond soldier in the glittering uniform. "Where do you find authority
for it?"

"Oh, perfectly right, colonel. In fact, for six
years past I've never seen it done any other
way. You'll find the authority on page 562,
Field Artillery Tactics of 1864."

For a moment Brax was dumb; he had long
heard of Cram as an expert in his own branch
of the service; but presently he burst forth:

"Well, in *our* tactics there's reason for every

blessed thing we do, but I'll be dinged if I can see rhyme or reason in such a formation as that. Why, sir, your one company takes up more room than my six,—makes twice as much of a show. Of course if a combined review is to show off the artillery it's all very well. However, go ahead, if you think you're right, sir; go ahead! I'll inquire into this later."

"I know we're right, colonel; and as for the reason, you'll see it when you open ranks for review and we come to 'action front:' then our line will be exactly that of the infantry. Meantime, sir, it isn't for us to go ahead. We've gone as far as we can until your adjutant makes the next move."

But Braxton had ridden away disgusted before Cram wound up his remarks.

"Go on, Major Minor; just run this thing without reference to the battery. Damned if I understand their methods. Let Cram look after his own affairs; if he goes wrong, why—it's none of our concern."

And so Minor had nodded "Go ahead" to Mr. Drake, and presently the whole command made its bow, so to speak, to Minor as its immediate chief, and then he drew sword and his untried

voice became faintly audible. The orders "Pre-
pare for review" and "To the rear open order"
were instantly followed by a stentorian "Action
front" down at the left, the instant leap and rush
of some thirty nimble cannoneers, shouts of
"Drive on!" the cracking of whips, the thunder
and rumble of wheels, the thud of plunging
hoofs. Forty-eight mettlesome horses in teams
of two abreast went dancing briskly away to
the rear, at sight of which Minor dropped his
jaw and the point of his sword and sat gazing
blankly after them, over the bowed head of his
placid sorrel, wondering what on earth it meant
that they should all be running away at the very
instant when he expected them to brace up for
review. But before he could give utterance to
his thoughts eight glossy teams in almost simul
taneous sweep to the left about came sharply
around again. The black muzzles of the guns
were pointed to the front, every axle exactly in
the prolongation of his front rank, every little
group of red-topped, red-trimmed cannoneers
standing erect and square, the chiefs of section
and of pieces sitting like statues on their handsome horses, the line of limbers accurately
covering the guns, and, still farther back, Mr.

c   d   5

Pierce could be heard shouting his orders for the alignment of the caissons. In the twinkling of an eye the rush and thunder were stilled, the battery without the twitch of a muscle stood ready for review, and old Brax, sitting in saddle at the reviewing point, watching the stirring sight with gloomy and cynical eye, was chafed still more to hear in a silvery voice from the group of ladies the unwelcome words, " Oh, wasn't that pretty!" He meant with all his heart to pull in some of the plumage of those confounded "woodpeckers," as he called them, before the day was over.

In grim silence, therefore, he rode along the front of the battalion, taking little comfort in the neatness of their quaint old-fashioned garb, the single-breasted, long-skirted frock-coats, the bulging black felt hats looped up on one side and decked with skimpy black feather, the glistening shoulder-scales and circular breastplates, the polish of their black leather belts, cartridge- and cap-boxes and bayonet-scabbards. It was all trim and soldierly, but he was bottling up his sense of annoyance for the benefit of Cram and his people. Yet what could he say? Neither he nor Minor had ever before been brought into such relations with the light artillery, and he simply didn't know where to hit. Lots of things looked queer, but after this initial experience he felt it best to say nothing until he could light on a point that no one could gainsay, and he found it in front of the left section.

"Where is Mr. Waring, sir?" he sternly asked.

"I wish I knew, colonel. His horse came back without him, as you doubtless saw, and, as he hasn't appeared, I'm afraid of accident."

"How did he come to leave his post, sir? I have no recollection of authorizing anything of the kind."

"Certainly not, colonel. He rode back to his quarters with my consent before adjutant's call had sounded, and he should have been with us again in abundant time."

"That young gentleman needs more discipline than he is apt to receive at this rate, Captain Cram, and I desire that you pay closer attention to his movements than you have done in the past.—Mr. Drake," he said to his adjutant, who was tripping around after his chief afoot, "call on Mr. Waring to explain his absence in writing and without delay.—This indifference to duty is

something to which I am utterly unaccustomed,"
continued Braxton, again addressing Cram, who
preserved a most uncompromising serenity of
countenance; and with this parting shot the
colonel turned gruffly away and soon retook his
station at the reviewing point.

Then came the second hitch. Minor had had
no experience whatever, as has been said, and
he first tried to wheel into column of companies
without closing ranks, whereupon every captain
promptly cautioned "Stand fast," and thereby
banished the last remnant of Minor's senses.
Seeing that something was wrong, he tried
again, this time prefacing with "Pass in review," and still the captains were implacable.
The nearest one, in a stage whisper, tried to
make the major hear "Close order, first." But
all the time Brax was losing more of his temper
and Minor what was left of his head, and Brax
came down like the wolf on the fold, gave the
command to "Close order" himself, and was
instantly echoed by Cram's powerful shout
"Limber to the rear," followed by "Pieces left
about! Caissons forward!" Then in the rumble and clank of the responding battery, Minor's
next command was heard by only the right

wing of the battalion, and the company wheels
were ragged. So was the next part of the performance when he started to march in review,
never waiting, of course, for the battery to
wheel into column of sections. This omission,
however, in no wise disconcerted Cram, who,
following at rapid walk, soon gained on the rear
of column, passing his post commander in beautiful order and with most accurate salute on the
part of himself and officers, and, observing this,
Minor took heart, and, recovering his senses to
a certain extent, gave the command "Guide
left" in abundant time to see that the new
guides were accurately in trace, thereby insur-
ing what he expected to find a beautiful wheel
into line to the left, the commands for which
movement he gave in louder and more confident
tone, but was instantly nonplussed by seeing the
battery wheel into line to the *right* and move off
in exactly the opposite direction from what he
had expected. This was altogether too much
for his equanimity. Digging his spurs into the
flanks of the astonished sorrel, he darted off
after Cram, waving his sword, and shouting,—

"*Left* into line wheel, captain. *Left* into line
wheel."

In vain Mr. Pierce undertook to explain matters. Minor presumed that the artilleryman had made an actual blunder and was only enabled to correct it by a countermarch, and so rode back to his position in front of the centre of the reforming line, convinced that at last he had caught the battery commander.

When Braxton, therefore, came down to make his criticisms and comments upon the conduct of the review, Minor was simply amazed to find that instead of being in error Cram had gone exactly right and as prescribed by his drill regulations in wheeling to the right and gaining ground to the rear before coming up on the line. He almost peevishly declared that he wished the colonel, if he proposed having a combined review, would assume command himself, as he didn't care to be bothered with combination tactics of which he had never had previous knowledge. Being of the same opinion, Braxton himself took hold, and the next performance, though somewhat erroneous in many respects, was a slight improvement on the first, though Braxton did not give time for the battery to complete one movement before he would rush it into another. When the officers

assembled to compare notes during the rest
after the second repetition, Minor growled that
this was "a little better, yet not good," which
led to some one suggesting in low tone that the
major got his positives and comparatives worse
mixed than his tactics, and inquiring further
"whether it might not be well to dub him
Minor Major." The laughter that followed this
sally naturally reached the ears of the seniors,
and so Brax never let up on the command until
the review went off without an error of any
appreciable weight, without, in fact, "a hitch in
the fut or an unhitch in the harse," as Doyle expressed it. It was high noon when the battalion
got back to barracks and the officers hung out
their moist clothing to dry in the sun. It was
near one when the batterymen, officers and all,
came steaming up from the stables, and there
was the colonel's orderly with the colonel's compliments and desires to see Captain Cram before
the big batteryman had time to change his dress.

Braxton's first performance on getting into
cool habiliments was to go over to his office
and hunt through the book-shelves for a volume
in which he never before had felt the faintest
interest,—the Light Artillery Tactics of 1864.

There on his desk lay a stack of mail unopened, and Mr. Drake was already silently inditing the summary note to the culprit Waring. Brax wanted first to see with his own eyes the instructions for light artillery when reviewed with other troops, vaguely hoping that there might still be some point on which to catch his foeman on the hip. But if there were he did not find it. He was tactician enough to see that even if Cram had formed with his leading drivers on line with the infantry, as Braxton thought he should have done, neither of the two methods of forming into battery would then have got his guns where they belonged. Cram's interpretation of the text was backed by the custom of service, and there was no use criticising it further. And so, after discontentedly hunting through the dust-covered pages awhile in hopes of stumbling on some codicil or rebuttal, the colonel shut it with a disgusted snap and tossed the offending tome on the farthest table. At that moment Brax could have wished the board of officers who prepared the Light Artillery Tactics in the nethermost depths of the neighboring swamp. Then he turned on his silent staff officer,—a not unusual expedient.

" Why on earth, Mr. Drake, didn't you look up that point, instead of making such a break before the whole command?"

" I couldn't find anything about it in Casey, sir, anywhere," replied the perturbed young man. " I didn't know where else to look."

" Well, you might have asked Mr. Ferry or Mr. Pierce. The Lord knows you waste enough time with 'em."

" *You* might have asked Captain Cram," was what Drake wanted to say, but wisely did not. He bit the end of his penholder instead, and bridled his tongue and temper.

".The next time I have a review with a mounted battery, by George!" said the post commander, finally, bringing his fist down on the table with a crash, " I just—won't have it."

He had brought down the pile of letters as well as his fist, and Drake sprang to gather them, replacing them on the desk and dexterously slipping a paper-cutter under the flap of each envelope as he did so. At the very first note he opened, Brax threw himself back in his chair with a long whistle of mingled amazement and concern, then turned suddenly on his adjutant.

"What became of Mr. Waring? He wasn't hurt?"

"Not a bit, sir, that I know of. He drove to town with Captain Cram's team,—at least I was told so,—and left that note for you there, sir."

"He did!—left the post and left a note for me? Why!——" But here Braxton broke off short, tore open the note, and read:

"MY DEAR COLONEL,—I trust you will overlook the informality of my going to town without previously consulting you. I had purposed, of course, asking your permission, but the mishap that befell me in the runaway of my horse prevented my appearance at the review, and had I waited your return from the field it would have compelled me to break my engagement with our friends the Allertons. Under the circumstances I felt sure of your complaisance.

"As I hope to drive Miss Allerton down after the *matinée,* might it not be a good idea to have dress-parade and the band out? They have seen the battery drills, but are much more desirous of seeing the infantry.

"Most sincerely yours,
"S. G. WARING."

"Well, for consummate impudence this beats the Jews!" exclaimed Brax. "Orderly, my compliments to Captain Cram, and say I wish to see him at once, if he's back from stables."

Now, as has been said, Cram had had no time to change to undress uniform, but Mrs. Cram had received the orderly's message, had informed that martial Mercury that the captain was not yet back from stables, and that she would tell him at once on his return. Well she knew that mischief was brewing, and her woman's wit was already enlisted in behalf of her friend. Hurriedly pencilling a note, she sent a messenger to her liege, still busy with his horses, to bid him come to her, if only for a moment, on his way to the office. And when he came, heated, tired, but bubbling over with eagerness to tell her of the fun they had been having with Brax, she met him with a cool tankard of "shandygaff," which he had learned to like in England among the horse-artillery fellows, and declared the very prince of drinks after active exercise in hot weather. He quaffed it eagerly, flung off his shako and kissed her gratefully, and burst all at once into laughing narration of the morning's work, but she checked him:

"Ned, dear, don't stop for that yet. I know you're too full of tact to let Colonel Braxton see it was any fun for you, and he's waiting at the office. Something tells me it's about Mr. Waring. Now put yourself in Mr. Waring's place. Of course he ought never to have made that engagement until he had consulted you, but he never dreamed that there would be a review to-day, and so he invited the Allertons to break-fast with him at Moreau's and go to the *matinée.*"

"Why, that rascal Ananias said it was to breakfast at the general's," interrupted the battery commander.

"Well, perhaps he was invited there too. I believe I did hear something of that. But he had made this arrangement with the Allertons. Now, of course, if review were over at ten he could just about have time to dress and catch the eleven-o'clock car, but that would make it very late, and when Bay Billy broke away from Ananias nobody could catch him for over half an hour. Mr. Ferry had taken the section, Mr. Waring wasn't needed, and—— Why, Ned, when I drove in, fearing to find him injured, and saw him standing there the picture of con-sternation and despair, and he told me about his engagement, I said myself, 'Why don't you go now?' I told him it was what you surely would say if you were here. Neither of us thought the colonel would object, so long as you approved, and he wrote such a nice note. Why, Ned, he only just had time to change his dress and drive up with Jeffers——"

"With Jeffers? With my—er—our team and wagon? Well, I like——"

"Of course you like it, you old darling. She's such a dear girl, though just a little bit gushing, you know. Why, I said, certainly the team should go. But, Ned, here's what I'm afraid of. Mrs. Braxton saw it drive in at nine-thirty, just after Billy ran away, and she asked Jeffers who was going, and he told her Mr. Waring, and she has told the colonel, I'll wager. Now, what you have got to do is to explain that to him, so that he won't blame Mr. Waring."

"The dickens I have! The most barefaced piece of impudence even Sam Waring was ever guilty of—to me, at least, though I've no doubt he's done worse a dozen times. Why, bless your heart, Nell, how can I explain? You might, but——"

"But would you have me suppose my big

6

soldier couldn't handle that matter as well as I?
No, sir! Go and do it, sir. And, mind you,
I'm going to invite them all up here to the gal-
lery to hear the band play and have a cup of tea
and a nibble when they come down this evening.
He's going to drive the Allertons here."

"Worse and more of it! Why, you con-
spiracy in petticoats, you'll be the ruin of me!
Old Brax is boiling over now. If he dreams
that Waring has been taking liberties with him
he'll fetch him up so short——"

"Exactly! You mustn't let him. You must
tell him I sent him up with your team—yours,
mind you—to keep his engagement, since it
was impossible for him to come back to review ground. Of course he wouldn't expect
him to appear afoot."

"Don't know about that, Nell. I reckon
that's the way he'll order out the whole gang
of us next time. He's had his fill of mounted
work to-day."

"Well, if he should, you be sure to acquiesce
gracefully now. Whatsoever you do, don't let
him put Mr. Waring in arrest while Gwen
Allerton is here. It would spoil—everything."

"Oh, match-making, is it? Then I'll try."

And so, vexed, but laughing, half indignant, yet wholly subordinate to the whim of his beloved better half, the captain hastened over, and found Colonel Braxton sitting with gloomy brow at his littered desk, his annoyance of the morning evidently forgotten in matters more serious.

"Oh—er—Cram, come in, come in, man," said he, distractedly. "Here's a matter I want to see you about. It's—well, just take that letter and read. Sit down, sit down. Read, and tell me what we ought to do about it."

And as Cram's blue eyes wandered over the written page they began to dilate. He read from start to finish, and then dropped his head into his hand, his elbow on his knee, his face full of perplexity and concern.

"What do you think of it? Is there any truth——" and the colonel hesitated.

"As to their being seen together, perhaps. As to the other,—the challenge,—I don't believe it."

"Well, Cram, this is the second or third letter that has come to me in the same hand. Now, you must see to it that he returns and doesn't quit the post until this matter is arranged."

"I'll attend to it, sir," was the answer.

And so that evening, while Waring was slowly driving his friends about the shaded roads under the glistening white pillars of the rows of officers' quarters, chatting joyously with them and describing the objects so strange to their eyes, Mrs. Cram's " little foot-page" came to beg that they should alight a few minutes and take a cup of tea. They could not. The Allertons were engaged, and it was necessary to drive back at once to town, but they stopped for a moment to chat with their pretty hostess under the gallery, and then a moment later, as they rolled out of the resounding sally-port, an orderly ran up, saluted, and slipped a note in Waring's hand.

" It is immediate, sir," was his explanation.

" Ah! Miss Allerton, will you pardon me one moment?" said Waring, as he shifted whip and reins into the left hand and turned coolly up the levee road. Then with the right he forced open and held up the missive.

It only said, " Whatsoever you do, be here before taps to-night. Come direct to me, and I will explain.

> " Your friend,
> " CRAM."

"All right," said Waring, aloud. "My compliments to the captain, and say I'll be with him."

But even with this injunction he failed to appear. Midnight came without a word from Waring, and the morning dawned and found him absent still.

CHAPTER III.

It was one of Sam Waring's oddities that, like the hero of "Happy Thoughts," other people's belongings seemed to suit him so much better than his own. The most immaculately dressed man in the regiment, he was never satisfied with the result of the efforts of the New York artists whom he favored with his custom and his criticism. He would wear three or four times a new coat just received from that metropolis, and spend not a little time, when not on duty or in uniform, in studying critically its cut and fit in the various mirrors that hung about his bachelor den, gayly humming some operatic air as he conducted the survey, and generally winding up with a wholesale denunciation of the cutter and an order to Ananias to go over and get some other fellow's coat, that he might try the effect of that. These were liberties he took only with his chums and intimates, to be sure, but they were liberties all the same, and it

was delicious to hear the laugh with which he
would tell how Pierce had to dress in uniform
when he went up to the opera Thursday night,
or how, after he had worn Ferry's stylish morning suit to make a round of calls in town and
that young gentleman later on went up to see
a pretty girl in whom he felt a growing interest, her hateful little sister had come in and
commented on his "borrowing Mr. Waring's
clothes." No man in the battery would ever
think of refusing Sam the use of anything he
possessed, and there were half a dozen young
fellows in the infantry who were just as ready
to pay tribute to his whims. Nor was it among
the men alone that he found such indulgence.
Mrs. Cram had not known him a fortnight
when, with twinkling eyes and a betraying
twitch about the corners of his mouth, he appeared one morning to say he had invited some
friends down to luncheon at the officers' mess
and the mess had no suitable china, therefore he
would thank her to send over hers, also some
table-cloths and napkins, and forks and spoons.
When the Forty-Sixth Infantry were on their
way to Texas and the officers' families were
entertained over-night at the barracks and his

rooms were to be occupied by the wife, sister,
and daughters of Captain Craney, Waring sent
the battery team and spring wagon to town with
a note to Mrs. Converse, of the staff, telling her
the ladies had said so much about the lovely
way her spare rooms were furnished that he had
decided to draw on her for wash-bowls, pitchers,
mosquito-frames, nets and coverlets, blankets,
pillows, slips, shams, and anything else she
might think of. And Mrs. Converse loaded up
the wagon accordingly. This was the more
remarkable in her case because she was one of
the women with whom he had never yet danced,
which was tantamount to saying that in the
opinion of this social bashaw Mrs. Converse was
not considered a good partner, and, as the lady
entertained very different views on that subject
and was passionately fond of dancing, she had
resented not a little the line thus drawn to her
detriment. She not only loaned, however, all
he asked for, but begged to be informed if
there were not something more she could do to
help entertain his visitors. Waring sent her
some lovely flowers the next week, but failed to
take her out even once at the staff german.
Mrs. Cram was alternately aghast and delighted

at what she perhaps justly called his incomparable impudence. They were coming out of church together one lovely morning during the winter. There was a crowd in the vestibule. Street dresses were then worn looped, yet there was a sudden sound of rip, rent, and tear, and a portly woman gathered up the trailing skirt of a costly silken gown and whirled with annihilation in her eyes upon the owner of the offending foot.

"That is far too elegant a skirt to be worn unlooped, madame," said Mrs. Cram's imperturbable escort, in his most suave and dulcet tones, lifting a glossy silk hat and bowing profoundly. And Mrs. Cram laughed all the way back to barracks at the recollection of the utter discomfiture in the woman's face.

These are mere specimen bricks from the fabric which Waring had builded in his few months of artillery service. The limits of the story are all too contracted to admit of extended detail. So, without further expansion, it may be said that when he drove up to town on this eventful April day in Cram's wagon and Larkin's hat and Ferry's Hatfield clothes, with Pierce's precious London umbrella by his side

and Merton's watch in his pocket, he was as
stylish and presentable a fellow as ever issued
from a battery barrack, and Jeffers, Cram's
English groom, mutely approved the general
appearance of his prime favorite among the
officers at the post, at most of whom he opened
his eyes in cockney amaze, and critically noted
the skill with which Mr. Waring tooled the
spirited bays along the levee road.

Nearly a mile above the barracks, midway
between the long embankment to their left and
the tall white picket fence surmounted by the
olive-green foliage of magnolias and orange-
trees on the other hand, they had come upon
a series of deep mud-holes in the way, where
the seepage-water from the rapidly-rising flood
was turning the road-way into a pond. Stuck
helplessly in the mud, an old-fashioned cabri-
olet was halted. Its driver was out and up
to his knees thrashing vainly at his straining,
staggering horse. The tortuous road-way was
blocked, but Waring had been up and down
the river-bank too many times both day and
night to be daunted by a matter so trivial. He
simply cautioned Jeffers to lean well over the
inner wheel, guided his team obliquely up the

slope of the levee, and drove quietly along its
level top until abreast the scene of the wreck.
One glance into the interior of the cab caused
him suddenly to stop, to pass the reins back to
Jeffers, to spring down the slope until he stood
at the edge of the sea of mud. Here he raised
his hat and cried,—

"Madame Lascelles! madame! this is indeed
lucky—for me. Let me get you out."

At his call a slender, graceful woman who
was gazing in anxiety and dismay from the
opposite side of the cab and pleading with the
driver not to beat his horse, turned suddenly,
and a pair of lovely dark eyes lighted up at
sight of his face. Her pallor, too, gave instant
place to a warm flush. A pretty child at her
side clapped her little hands and screamed with
delight,—

"*Maman! maman! C'est M'sieu'* Vayreeng;
c'est Sa-am.*"

"Oh, Monsieur Wareeng! I'm so glad you've
come! Do speak to that man! It is horrible
the way he beat that poor horse.—*Mais non,*
Nin Nin!" she cried, reproving the child, now
stretching forth her little arms to her friend and
striving to rise and leap to him.

"I'd like to know how in hell I'm to get this cab out of such a hole as this if I don't beat him," exclaimed the driver, roughly. Then once more, "Dash blank dash your infernal hide! I'll learn you to balk with me again!" Then down came more furious lashes on the quivering hide, and the poor tortured brute began to back, thereby placing the frail four-wheeler in imminent danger of being upset.

"Steady there! Hold your hand, sir! Don't strike that horse again. Just stand at his head a moment and keep quiet till I get these ladies out," called Waring, in tone quiet yet commanding.

"I'll get 'em out myself in my own way, if they'll only stop their infernal yellin'," was the coarse reply.

"Oh, Monsieur Wareeng," exclaimed the lady in undertone, "the man has been drinking, I am sure. He has been so rude in his language."

Waring waited for no more words. Looking quickly about him, he saw a plank lying on the levee slope. This he seized, thrust one end across the muddy hole until it rested in the cab, stepped lightly across, took the child in his arms, bore her to the embankment and set her down, then sprang back for her young mother, who, trembling slightly, rose and took his outstretched hand just as another lash fell on the horse's back and another lurch followed. Waring caught at the cab-rail with one hand, threw the other arm about her slender waist, and, fairly lifting little Madame over the wheel, sprang with her to the shore, and in an instant more had carried her, speechless and somewhat agitated, to the top of the levee.

"Now," said he, "let me drive you and Nin Nin wherever you were going. Is it to market or church?"

"*Mais non*—to *bonne maman's*, of whom it is the *fête*," cried the eager little one, despite her mother's stern orders of silence. "Look!" she exclaimed, showing her dainty little legs and feet in creamy silken hose and kid.

It was "bonne maman," explained Madame, who had ordered the cab from town for them, never dreaming of the condition of the river road or suspecting that of the driver.

"So much the happier for me," laughed Waring.—"Take the front seat, Jeffers.—Now, Nin Nin, *ma fleurette*, up with you!" And the delighted child was lifted to her perch in the

D   7

stylish trap she had so often admired. "Now,
madame," he continued, extending his hand.

But Madame hung back, hesitant and blushing.

"Oh, Monsieur Wareeng, I cannot, I must
not. Is it not that some one shall extricate the
cab?"

"No one from this party, at least," laughed
Waring, mischievously making the most of her
idiomatic query. "Your driver is more *cochon*
than *cocher*, and if he drowns in that mud 'twill
only serve him right. Like your famous com-
patriot, he'll have a chance to say, 'I will drown,
and no one shall help me,' for all I care. The
brute! *Allons!* I will drive you to *bonne
maman's* of whom it is the *fête*. Bless that baby
daughter! And Madame d'Hervilly shall bless
Nin Nin's *tout dévoué* Sam."

And Madame Lascelles found further remon-
strance useless. She was lifted into the seat, by
which time the driver, drunken and truculent,
had waded after them.

"Who's to pay for this?" was his surly question.

"You, I fancy, as soon as your employer
learns of your driving into that hole," was
Waring's cool reply.

"Well, by God, I want five dollars for my fare and trouble, and I want it right off." And, whip in hand, the burly, mud-covered fellow came lurching up the bank. Across the boggy street beyond the white picket fence the green blinds of a chamber window in an old-fashioned Southern house were thrown open, and two feminine faces peered forth, interested spectators of the scene.

"Here, my man!" said Waring, in low tone, "you have earned no five dollars, and you know it. Get your cab out, come to Madame d'Hervilly's, where you were called, and whatever is your due will be paid you; but no more of this swearing or threatening,—not another word of it."

"I want my money, I say, and I mean to have it. I'm not talking to you; I'm talking to the lady that hired me."

"But I have not the money. It is for my mother—Madame d'Hervilly—to pay. You will come there."

"I want it now, I say. I've got to hire teams to get my cab out. I got stalled here carrying you and your child, and I mean to have my pay right now, or I'll know the reason why. Your

swell friend's got the money. It's none of my
business how you pay him."

But that ended the colloquy. Waring's fist
landed with resounding whack under the cabman's jaw, and sent him rolling down into the
mud below. He was up, floundering and furious, in less than a minute, cursing horribly and
groping in the pocket of his overcoat.

"It's a pistol, lieutenant. Look out!" cried
Jeffers.

There was a flash, a sharp report, a stifled cry
from the cab, a scream of terror from the child.
But Waring had leaped lightly aside, and before
the half-drunken brute could cock his weapon for
a second shot he was felled like a log, and the
pistol wrested from his hand and hurled across the
levee. Another blow crashed full in his face as he
strove to find his feet, and this time his muddled
senses warned him it were best to lie still.

Two minutes more, when he lifted his battered
head and strove to stanch the blood streaming
from his nostrils, he saw the team driving briskly
away up the crest of the levee; and, overcome
by maudlin contemplation of his foeman's triumph and his own wretched plight, the cabman
sat him down and wept aloud.

And to his succor presently there came ministering angels from across the muddy way, one
with a brogue, the other in a bandanna, and
between the two he was escorted across a dry
path to the magnolia-fringed enclosure, comforted with soothing applications without and
within, and encouraged to tell his tale of woe.
That he should wind it up with vehement expression of his ability to thrash a thousand
swells like the one who had abused him, and a
piratical prophecy that he'd drink his heart's
blood within the week, was due not so much to
confidence in his own powers, perhaps, as to the
strength of the whiskey with which he had been
liberally supplied.   Then the lady of the house
addressed her Ethiop maid-of-all-work:

"Go you over to Anatole's now, 'Louette.
Tell him if any of the byes are there I wahnt
'um.   If Dawson is there, from the adjutant's
office, I wahnt him quick.   Tell him it's Mrs.
Doyle, and never mind if he's been dhrinkin';
he shall have another dhrop here."

And at her beck there presently appeared
three or four besotted-looking specimens in the
coarse undress uniform of the day, poor devils,
absent without leave from their post below and

hoping only to be able to beg or steal whiskey enough to stupefy them before the patrol should come and drag them away to the guard-house. Promise of liberal reward in shape of liquor was sufficient to induce three of their number to go out with the fuming cabman and help rescue his wretched brute and trap. The moment they were outside the gate she turned on the fourth, a pallid, sickly man, whose features were delicate, whose hands were white and slender, and whose whole appearance, despite glassy eyes and tremulous mouth and limbs, told the pathetic story of better days.

"You're off ag'in, are you? Sure I heerd so, and you're mad for a dhrink now. Can ye write, Dawson, or must I brace you up furrst?"

An imploring look, an unsteady gesture, alone answered.

"Here, thin, wait! It's absinthe ye need, my buck. Go you into that room now and wash yourself, and I'll bring it, and whin the others come back for their whiskey I'll tell 'um you've gone. You're to do what I say, now, and Doyle will see you t'rough; if not, it's back to that hell in the guard-house you'll go, my word on it."

"Oh, for God's sake, Mrs. Doyle——" began the poor wretch, imploringly, but the woman shut him off.

"In there wid you! the others are coming." And, unbarring the front door, she presently admitted the trio returning to claim the fruits of their honest labor.

"Is he gone? Did he tell you what happened?"

"He's gone, yes," answered one: "he's gone to get square with the lieutenant and his cockney dog-robber. He says they both jumped on him and kicked his face in when he was down and unarmed and helpless. Was he lyin'?"

"Oh, they bate him cruel. But did he tell you of the lady—who it was they took from him?"

"Why, sure, the wife of that old Frenchman, Lascelles, that lives below,—her the lieutenant's been sparkin' this three months."

"The very wan, mind ye!" replied the lady of the house, with significant emphasis and glance from her bleary eyes; "the very wan," she finished, with slow nodding accompaniment of the frowzy head. "And that's the kind of gintlemen that undertakes to hold up their heads over soldiers like Doyle. Here, byes, dhrink now, but be off ag'inst his coming. He'll be here any minute. Take this to comfort ye, but kape still about this till ye see me ag'in—or Doyle. Now run." And with scant ceremony the dreary party was hustled out through a paved court-yard to a gate-way opening on a side street. Houses were few and scattering so far below the heart of the city. The narrow strip of land between the great river and the swamp was cut up into walled enclosures, as a rule,—abandoned warehouses and cotton-presses, moss-grown one-storied frame structures, standing in the midst of desolate fields and decrepit fences. Only among the peaceful shades of the Ursuline convent and the warlike flanking towers at the barracks was there aught that spoke of anything but demoralization and decay. Back from the levee a block or two the double lines of strap-iron stretched over a wooden causeway between parallel wet ditches gave evidence of some kind of a railway, on which, at rare intervals, jogged a sleepy mule with a sleepier driver and a musty old rattle-trap of a car,—a car butting up against the animal's lazy hocks and rousing him occasionally to ringing

and retaliatory kicks. Around the barracks the
buildings were closer, mainly in the way of sa-
loons; then came a mile-long northward stretch
of track. with wet fields on either side, fringed
along the river by solid structures and walled
enclosures that told of days more prosperous
than those which so closely followed the war.
It was to one of these graceless drinking-shops
and into the hands of a rascally " dago" known
as Anatole that Mrs. Doyle commended her trio
of allies, and being rid of them she turned back
to her prisoner, their erstwhile companion.
Absinthe wrought its work on his meek and
pliant spirit, and the shaking hand was nerved
to do the woman's work. At her dictation,
with such corrections as his better education
suggested, two letters were draughted, and with
these in her hand she went aloft. In fifteen
minutes she returned, placed one of these letters
in an envelope already addressed to Monsieur
Armand Lascelles, No. — Rue Royale, the other
she handed to Dawson. It was addressed in
neat and delicate feminine hand to Colonel
Braxton, Jackson Barracks.

" Now, Dawson, ye can't see her this day, and
she don't want ye till you can come over here

f

sober. Off wid ye now to barracks. They're
all out at inspection yet, and will be for an hour.
Lay this wid the colonel's mail on his desk, and
thin go you to your own.   Come to me this
afthernoon for more dhrink if ye can tell me
what he said and did when he read it. No! no
more liquor now. That'll brace ye till dinner-
time, and more would make ye dhrunk."

Miserably he plodded away down the levee,
while she, his ruler, throwing on a huge, dirty
white sun-bonnet, followed presently in his
tracks, and "shadowed" him until she saw him
safely reach the portals of the barracks after
one or two fruitless scouts into wayside bars in
hope of finding some one to treat or trust him
to a drink. Then, retracing her steps a few
blocks, she rang sharply at the lattice gate open
ing into a cool and shaded enclosure, beyond
which could be seen the white-pillared veranda
of a long, low, Southern homestead.   A grin
ning negro boy answered the summons.

"It's you, is it, Alphonse? Is your mistress
at home?"

"No; gone town,—*chez Madame d'Hervilly.*"

"Madame Devillcase, is it? Very well; you
skip to town wid that note and get it in your

master's hands before the cathedral clock strikes
twelve, or ye'll suffer. There's a car in t'ree
minutes."

And then, well content with her morning's
work, the consort of the senior first lieutenant
of Light Battery "X" (a dame whose creden-
tials were too clouded to admit of her reception
or recognition within the limits of a regular
garrison, where, indeed, to do him justice, Mr.
Doyle never wished to see her, or, for that
matter, anywhere else) betook herself to the
magnolia-shaded cottage where she dwelt beyond
the pale of military interference, and some hours
later sent 'Louette to say to Doyle she wanted
him, and Doyle obeyed. In his relief at finding
the colonel had probably forgotten the pecca-
dillo for which he expected punishment, in bliss-
ful possession of Mr. Waring's sitting-room and
supplies now that Waring was absent, the big
Irishman was preparing to spend the time in
drinking his junior's health and whiskey and
discoursing upon the enormity of his miscon-
duct with all comers, when Ananias entered
and informed him there was a lady below who
wished to see him,—"lady" being the euphem-
ism of the lately enfranchised for the females of

their race. It was 'Louette with the mandate
from her mistress, a mandate he dared not
disregard.

"Say I'll be along in a minute," was his
reply, but he sighed and swore heavily, as
he slowly reascended the stair. "Give me another dhrink, smut," he ordered Ananias, dis-
regarding Ferry's suggestion, "Better drink no
more till after dark." Then, swallowing his
potion, he went lurching down the steps without another word. Ferry and Pierce stepped
to the gallery and gazed silently after him as he
veered around to the gate leading to the old
war-hospital enclosure where the battery was
quartered. Already his walk was perceptibly
unsteady.

"Keeps his head pretty well, even after his
legs are gone," said Ferry. "Knows too much
to go by the sally-port. He's sneaking out
through the back gate."

"Why, what does he go out there for, when
he has the run of Waring's sideboard?"

"Oh, didn't you hear? Mrs. Doyle sent for
him."

"That's it, is it? Sometimes I wonder which
one of those two will kill the other."

"Oh, he wouldn't dare. That fellow is an abject coward in the dark. He believes in ghosts, spooks, banshees, and wraiths,—everything uncanny,—and she'd haunt him if he laid his hands on her. There's only one thing that he'd be more afraid of than Bridget Doyle living, and that would be Bridget Doyle dead."

"Why can't he get rid of her? What hold has she on him? This thing's an infernal scandal as it stands. She's only been here a month or so, and everybody in garrison knows all about her, and these doughboys don't make any bones about chaffing us on our lady friends."

"Well, everybody supposed he had got rid of her years ago. He shook her when he was made first sergeant, just before the war. Why, I've heard some of the old stagers say there wasn't a finer-looking soldier in all the regiment than Jim Doyle when he married that specimen at Brownsville. Doyle, too, supposed she was dead until after he got his commission, then she reappeared and laid claim to him. It would have been an easy enough matter five years ago to prove she had forfeited all rights, but now he can't. Then she's got some confounded hold on him, I don't know what, but it's killing the poor

8

beggar. Good thing for the regiment, though :
so let it go."

"Oh, I don't care a rap how soon we're rid
of him or her,—the sooner the better; only I
hate to hear these fellows laughing and sneering
about Mrs. Doyle." And here the young fellow
hesitated. "Ferry, you know I'm as fond of
Sam Waring as any of you. I liked him better
than any man in his class when we wore the
gray. When they were yearlings we were
plebes, and devilled and tormented by them
most unmercifully day and night. I took to
him then for his kindly, jolly ways. No one
ever knew him to say or do a cross or brutal
thing. I liked him more every year, and
missed him when he was graduated. I rejoiced
when he got his transfer to us. It's because
I like him so much that I hate to hear these
fellows making their little flings now."

"What flings?" said Ferry.

"Well, you know as much as I do. You've
heard as much, too, I haven't a doubt."

"Nobody's said anything about Sam Waring
in my hearing that reflected on him in any way
worth speaking of," said Ferry, yet not very
stoutly.

"Not on him so much, perhaps, as the world looks at this sort of thing, but on her. She's young, pretty, married to a man years her senior, a snuffy, frowzy old Frenchman. She's alone with her child and one or two servants from early morning till late evening, and with that weazened little monkey of a man the rest of the time. The only society she sees is the one or two gossipy old women of both sexes who live along the levee here. The only enjoyment she has is when she can get to her mother's up in town, or run up to the opera when she can get Lascelles to take her. That old mummy cares nothing for music and still less for the dance; she loves both, and so does Waring. *Monsieur le Mari* goes out into the foyer between the acts to smoke his cigarette and gossip with other relics like himself. Waring has never missed a night she happened to be there for the last six weeks. I admit he is there many a time when she is not, but after he's had a few words with the ladies in the general's box, what becomes of him? I don't know, because I'm seldom there, but Dryden and Taggart and Jack Merton of the infantry can tell you. He is sitting by her in the D'Hervilly *loge grillée* and going over the last act with her and rhapsodizing about Verdi, Bellini, Mozart, or Gounod,—Gounod especially and the garden-scene from 'Faust.'"

"Isn't her mother with her, and, being in mourning, doesn't she have to stay in her latticed loge instead of promenading in the foyer and drinking that two-headaches-for-a-picayune punch?" queried Ferry, eager for a diversion.

"Suppose she is," answered Pierce, stoutly. "I'm a crank,—strait-laced, if you like. It's the fault of my bringing up. But I know, and you know, that that little woman, in her loneliness and in her natural longing for some congenial spirit to commune with, is simply falling madly in love with Sam Waring, and there will be tragedy here before we can stop it."

"See here, Pierce," asked Ferry, "do you suppose Mrs. Cram would be so loyal a friend to Waring if she thought there was anything wrong in his attentions to Madame Lascelles? Do you suppose Cram himself wouldn't speak?"

"He has spoken."

"He has? To whom?"

"To me, three days ago; said I had known

Waring longest and best, perhaps was his most
intimate friend, and he thought I ought to warn
him of what people were saying."

"What have you done?"

"Nothing yet: simply because I know Sam
Waring so well that I know just what he'd do,
—go and pull the nose of the man who gossiped
about him and her. Then we'd have a fight on
our hands."

"Well, we can fight, I suppose, can't we?"

"Not without involving a woman's name."

"Oh, good Lord, Pierce, was there ever a row
without a woman *au fond?*"

"That's a worm-eaten witticism, Ferry, and
you're too decent a fellow, as a rule, to be
cynical. I've got to speak to Waring, and I
don't know how to do it. I want your advice."

"Well, my advice is *Punch's:* Don't. Hello!
here's Dryden. Thought you were on court
duty up at head-quarters to-day, old man.
Come in and have a wet?" Mr. Ferry had
seen some happy days at Fortress Monroe when
the ships of Her Majesty's navy lay off the
Hygeia and the gallants of England lay to at
the bar, and Ferry rejoiced in the vernacular of

the United Service, so far as he could learn it, as practised abroad.

"Thanks. Just had one over at Merton's. Hear you've been having review and all that sort of thing down here," said the infantryman, as he lolled back in an easy-chair and planted his boot-heels on the gallery rail. "Glad I got out of it. Court met and adjourned at ten, so I came home. How'd Waring get off?"

"Huh!—Cram's wagon," laughed Ferry, rather uncomfortably, however.

"Oh, Lord, yes, I know that. Didn't I see him driving Madame Lascelles up Rampart Street as I came down in the mule-car?"

And then Pierce and Ferry looked at each other, startled.

That evening, therefore, it was a comfort to both when Sam came tooling the stylish turnout through the sally-port and his battery chums caught sight of the Allertons. Pierce was just returning from stables, and Ferry was smoking a pipe of *perique* on the broad gallery, and both hastened to don their best jackets and doff their best caps to these interesting and interested callers. Cram himself had gone off for a ride and a think. He always declared his ideas were clearer after a gallop. The band played charmingly. The ladies came out and made a picturesque croquet-party on the green carpet of the parade. The officers clustered about and offered laughing wagers on the game. A dozen romping children were playing joyously around the tall flag-staff. The air was rich with the fragrance of the magnolia and Cape jasmine, and glad with music and soft and merry voices. Then the stirring bugles rang out their lively summons to the batterymen beyond the wall. The drums of the infantry rolled and rattled their echoing clamor. The guard sprang into ranks, and their muskets, glistening in the slanting beams of the setting sun, clashed in simultaneous "present" to the red-sashed officer of the day, and that official raised his plumed hat to the lieutenant with the lovely girl by his side and the smiling elders on the back seat as the team once more made the circuit of the post on the back trip to town, and Miss Flora Allerton clasped her hands and looked enthusiastically up into her escort's face.

" Oh," she cried, "isn't it all just too lovely for anything! Why, I think your life here must be like a dream."

But Miss Allerton, as Mrs. Cram had said, sometimes gushed, and life at Jackson Barracks was no such dream as it appeared.

The sun went down red and angry far across the tawny flood of the rushing river. The night lights were set at the distant bend below. The stars came peeping through a shifting filmy veil. The big trees on the levee and about the flanking towers began to whisper and complain and creak, and the rising wind sent long wisps of straggly cloud racing across the sky. The moon rose pallid and wan, hung for a while over the dense black mass of moss-grown cypress in the eastward swamp, then hid her face behind a heavy bank of clouds, as though reluctant to look upon the wrath to come, for a storm was rising fast and furious to break upon and deluge old Jackson Barracks.

Florence B. Johnson

CHAPTER IV.

WHEN Jeffers came driving into barracks on his return from town, his first care, as became the trained groom, was for his horses, and he was rubbing them down and bedding their stalls for the night when the sergeant of the battery guard, lantern in hand, appeared at the door. It was not yet tattoo, but by this time the darkness was intense, the heavens were hid, and the wind was moaning about the stables and gunshed and whistling away over the dismal expanse of flat, wet, ditch-tangled fields towards the swamp. But the cockney's spirits were blithe as the clouds were black. As was usual when he or any other servitor was in attendance on Waring, the reward had been munificent. He had lunched at Cassidy's at the lieutenant's expense while that officer and his friends were similarly occupied at the more exclusive Moreau's. He had stabled the team at the quartermaster's while he had personally attended the

matinée at the St. Charles, which was more to
his taste than Booth and high tragedy. He had
sauntered about the Tattersalls and smoked
Waring's cigars and patronized the jockeys
gathered there for the spring meeting on the
Metairie, but promptly on time was awaiting the
return of the party from their drive and lolling
about the ladies' entrance to the St. Charles
Hotel, when he became aware, as the lamps
were being lighted and the dusk of the evening
gave place to lively illumination, that two men
had passed and repassed the open portals several times, and that they were eying him curiously, and chattering to each other in French.
One of them he presently recognized as the
little "frog-eater" who occupied the old house
on the levee, Lascelles, the husband of the
pretty Frenchwoman he and the lieutenant had
dragged out of the mud that very morning and
had driven up to the old D'Hervilly place on
Rampart Street. Even as he was wondering
how cabby got out of his scrape and chuckling
with satisfaction over the scientific manner in
which Mr. Waring had floored that worthy,
Mr. Jeffers was surprised to find himself most
civilly accosted by old Lascelles, who had been

informed, he said, by Madame his wife, of the heroic services rendered her that morning by Monsieur Jeffers and Monsieur le Capitaine. He begged of the former the acceptance of the small *douceur* which he slipped into the Englishman's accustomed palm, and inquired when he might hope to see the brave captain and disembarrass himself of his burden of gratitude.

"Here they come now," said Jeffers, promptly pocketing the money and springing forward to knuckle his hat-brim and stand at the horses' heads. All grace and animation, Mr. Waring had assisted his friends to alight, had promised to join them in the ladies' parlor in ten minutes, had sprung to the seat again, signalling Jeffers to tumble up behind, and then had driven rapidly away through Carondelet Street to the broad avenue beyond. Here he tossed the reins to Jeffers, disappeared a moment, and came back with a little Indian-made basket filled to overflowing with exquisite double violets rich with fragrance.

"Give this to Mrs. Cram for me, and tell the captain I'll drop in to thank him in a couple of hours, and—— Here, Jeffers," he said, and Jeffers had pocketed another greenback, and

had driven briskly homeward, well content with
the result of his day's labors, and without having mentioned to Mr. Waring the fact that
Lascelles had been at the hotel making inquiries
for him. A day so profitable and so pleasant
Jeffers had not enjoyed since his arrival at the
barracks, and he was humming away in high
good humor, all reckless of the rising storm,
when the gruff voice of Sergeant Schwartz disturbed him:

"Chevvers, you will rebort at vonst to Captain Cram."

"Who says I will?" said Jeffers, cheerfully,
though bent on mischief, but was awed into
instant silence at seeing that veteran step
quickly back, stand attention, and raise his hand
in salute, for there came Cram himself, Pierce
with him.

"Did Mr. Waring come back with you?" was
the first question.

"No, sir; Hi left Mr. Warink on Canal
Street. 'E said 'e'd be back to thank the capt'in
in a little while, sir, and 'e sent these for the
capt'in's lady."

Cram took the beautiful basket of violets with
dubious hand, though his eyes kindled when

he noted their profusion and fragrance. Nell loved violets, and it was like Waring to remember so bountifully her fondness for them.

"What detained him? Did he send no word?"

"'E said nothink, and sent nothink but the basket, sir. 'E said a couple of hours, now I think of it, sir. 'E was going back to the 'otel to dine with a lady and gent."

For a moment Cram was silent. He glanced at Pierce, as much as to say, Have you no question to ask? but the youngster held his peace. The senior officer hated to inquire of his servant into the details of the day's doings. He was more than half indignant at Waring for having taken such advantage of even an implied permission as to drive off with his equipage and groom in so summary a way. Of course Nell had said, Take it and go, but Nell could have had no idea of the use to which the wagon was to be put. If Waring left the garrison with the intention of using the equipage to take Madame Lascelles driving, it was the most underhand and abominable thing he had ever heard of his doing. It was unlike him. It couldn't be true. Yet had not Braxton shown him the letter which said he was seen on the levee with her by his side? Had not Dryden further informed every man and woman and child with whom he held converse during the day that he had seen Waring with Cram's team driving Madame Lascelles up Rampart Street, and was not there a story already afloat that old Lascelles had forbidden him ever to darken his threshold again, —forbidden Madame to drive, dance, or even speak with him? And was there not already in the post commander's hand a note intimating that Monsieur Lascelles would certainly challenge Waring to instant and mortal combat if Waring had used the wagon as alleged? Jeffers must know about it, and could and should tell if required, but Cram simply could not and would not ask the groom to detail the movements of the gentleman. Had not Waring sent word he would be home in two hours and would come to see his battery commander at once? Did not that mean he would explain fully? Cram gulped down the query that rose to his lips.

"All right, then, Pierce; we'll take these over to Mrs. Cram and have a bite ready for Waring on his return," said the stout-hearted fellow, and, in refusing to question his servant, missed the chance of averting catastrophe.

And so they bore the beautiful cluster of violets, with its mute pledge of fidelity and full explanation, to his rejoicing Nell, and the trio sat and chatted, and one or two visitors came in for a while and then scurried home as the rain began to plash on the windows, and the bugles and drums and fifes sounded far away at tattoo and more than usually weird and mournful at taps, and finally ten-thirty came, by which time it had been raining torrents, and the wind was lashing the roaring river into foam, and the trees were bowing low before their master, and the levee road was a quagmire, and Cram felt convinced no cab could bring his subaltern home. Yet in his nervousness and anxiety he pulled on his boots, threw his gum coat over his uniform, tiptoed in to bend over Nell's sleeping form and whisper, should she wake, that he was going only to the sally-port or perhaps over to Waring's quarters, but she slept peacefully and never stirred, so noiselessly he slipped out on the gallery and down the stairs and stalked boldly out into the raging storm, guided by the dim light burning in Waring's room. Ananias was sleeping curled up on a rug in front of the open fireplace, and Cram stirred him up with his foot. The negro rolled lazily over, with a stretch and yawn.

"Did Mr. Waring take any arms with him?" queried the captain.

"Any whut, suh?" responded Ananias, rubbing his eyes and still only half awake.

"Any pistol or knife?"

"Lord, suh, no. Mr. Waring don't never carry anything o' dat sort."

A student-lamp was burning low on the centre-table. There lay among the books and papers a couple of letters, evidently received that day, and still unopened. There lay Waring's cigar-case, a pretty trifle given him by some far-away friend, with three or four fragrant Havanas temptingly visible. There lay a late magazine, its pages still uncut. Cram looked at the dainty wall clock, ticking merrily away over the mantel. Eleven-thirty-five! Well, he was too anxious to sleep anyhow, why not wait a few minutes? Waring might come, probably would come. If no cab could make its way down by the levee road, there were the late cars from town; they had to make the effort anyhow. Cram stepped to the sideboard, mixed a mild toddy, sipped it reflectively, then lighted a cigar and threw himself into the easy-chair. Ananias, meantime, was up and astir. Seeing that Cram was looking about in search of a paper-cutter, the boy stepped forward and bent over the table.

"De lieutenant always uses dis, suh," said he, lifting first one paper, then another, searching under each. "Don't seem to be yer now, suh. You've seen it, dough, captain,—dat cross-handled dagger wid de straight blade."

"Yes, I know. Where is it?" asked Cram. "That'll do."

"Tain't yer, suh, now. Can't find it yer, nohow."

"Well, then, Mr. Waring probably took a knife, after all."

"No, suh, I don't t'ink so. I never knowed him to use it befo' away from de room."

"Anybody else been here?" said Cram.

"Oh, dey was all in yer, suh, dis arternoon, but Mr. Doyle he was sent for, suh, and had to go."

A step and the rattle of a sword were heard on the gallery without. The door opened, and

in came Morton of the infantry, officer of the
day.

"Hello, Waring!" he began. "Oh, it's you,
is it, captain? Isn't Waring back? I saw the
light, and came up to chin with him a moment.
Beastly night, isn't it?"

"Waring isn't back yet. I look for him
by the eleven-thirty car," answered the captain.

"Why, that's in. No Waring there, but half
a dozen poor devils, half drowned and half
drunk, more'n half drunk, one of your men
among 'em. We had to put him into the guard-
house to keep him from murdering Dawson, the
head-quarters clerk. There's been some kind
of a row."

"Sorry to hear that. Who is the man?"

"Kane. He said Dawson was lying about his
officer and he wouldn't stand it."

"Kane!" exclaimed Cram, rising. "Why,
he's one of our best. I never heard of his being
riotous before."

"He's riotous enough to-night. He wanted
to lick all six of our fellows, and if I hadn't got
there when I did they would probably have
kicked him into a pulp. All were drunk;

Kane, too, I should say; and as for Dawson, he was just limp."

"Would you mind going down and letting me talk with Kane a moment? I never knew him to be troublesome before, though he sometimes drank a little. He was on pass this evening."

"Well, it's raining cats and dogs, captain, but come along. If you can stand it I can."

A few minutes later the sergeant of the guard threw open one of the wooden compartments in the guard-house, and there sat Kane, his face buried in his hands.

"I ordered him locked in here by himself, because I feared our fellows would hammer him if he were turned in with them," explained Mr. Merton, and at sound of the voice the prisoner looked up and saw his commander, dripping with wet. Unsteadily he rose to his feet.

"Captain," he began, thickly, "I'd never have done it in the world, sir, but that blackguard was drunk, sir, and slandering my officer, and I gave him fair warning to quit or I'd hit him, but he kept on."

"Ye-es? And what did he say?"

"He said—I wouldn't believe it, sir—that Mr.

Doyle was that drunk that him and some other fellers had lifted him out of the mud and put him to bed up there at—up there at the house, sir, back of Anatole's place. I think the captain knows."

"Ah, you should have steered clear of such company, Kane. Did this happen at Anatole's saloon?"

"Yes, sir, and them fellers was making so much noise that the dago turned them all out and shut up the shop at eleven o'clock, and that's what made them follow me home in the car and abuse me all the way. I couldn't stand it, sir."

"You would only have laughed at them if your better judgment hadn't been ruined by liquor. Sorry for you, Kane, but you've been drinking just enough to be a nuisance, and must stay where you are for the night. They'll be sorry for what they said in the morning.—Did you lock up the others, Mr. Merton?" he asked, as they turned away.

"All but Dawson, sir. I took him over to the hospital and put a sentry over him. That fellow looks to be verging on jimjams, and I wouldn't be surprised if he'd been talking as

Kane says." Merton might have added, "and it's probably true," but courtesy to his battery friend forbade. Cram did add mentally something to the same effect, but loyalty to his arm of the service kept him silent. At the flag-staff the two officers stopped.

"Merton, oblige me by saying nothing as to the alleged language about Doyle, will you?"

"Certainly, captain. Good-night."

Then, as the officer of the day's lantern flickered away in one direction, Cram turned in the other, and presently went climbing up the stairs to the gallery leading to the quarters of his senior first lieutenant. A dim light was shining through the shutters. Cram knocked at the door; no answer. Opening it, he glanced in. The room was unoccupied. A cheap marine clock, ticking between the north windows over the wash-stand, indicated midnight, and the battery commander turned away in vexation of spirit. Lieutenant Doyle had no authority to be absent from the post.

It was still dark and storming furiously when the bugles of the battery sounded the reveille, and by the light of the swinging lanterns the men marched away in their canvas stable rig, looking like a column of ghosts. Yet, despite the gale and the torrents of rain, Pierce was in no wise surprised to find Cram at his elbow when the horses were led out to water.

"Groom in-doors this morning, Mr. Pierce. Is Waring home?"

"No, sir; Ananias told me when he brought me up my coffee."

"Hold the morning report, then, until I come to the office. I fear we have both first lieutenants to report absent to-day. You and I may have to go to town: so get your breakfast early. We will ride. I doubt if even an ambulance could get through. Tell me, Pierce, have you spoken to Waring about—about that matter we were discussing? Has he ever given you any idea that he had received warning of any kind from old Lascelles—or any of his friends?"

"No, sir. I've had no chance to speak, to be sure, and, so far as I could observe, he and Mr. Lascelles seemed on very excellent terms only a few days ago."

"Well, I wish I had spoken myself," said Cram, and turned away.

That morning, with two first lieutenants absent without leave, the report of Light Battery

"X" went into the adjutant's office just as its commander and his junior subaltern went out and silently mounted the dripping horses standing in front. The two orderlies, with their heads poked through the slit of their ponchos, briskly seated themselves in saddle, and then the colonel hurried forth just in time to hail,—

"Oh, Cram! one minute." And Cram reined about and rode to the side of the post commander, who stood under the shelter of the broad gallery.

"I wouldn't say anything about this to any one at head-quarters except Reynolds. There's no one else on the staff to whom Waring would apply, is there?"

"No one, sir. Reynolds is the only man I can think of."

"Will you send an orderly back with word as soon as you know?"

"Yes, sir, the moment I hear. And-d—shall I send you word from—there?"—and Cram nodded northward, and then, in a lower tone,— "as to Doyle?"

"Oh, damn Doyle! I don't care if he never ——" But here the commander of the post regained control of himself, and with parting wave of the hand turned back to his office.

Riding in single file up the levee, for the city road was one long pool, with the swollen river on their left, and the slanting torrents of rain obscuring all objects on the other hand, the party made its way for several squares without exchanging a word. Presently the leading file came opposite the high wall of the Lascelles place. The green latticed gate stood open,—an unusual thing,—and both officers bent low over their pommels and gazed along the dark, rain-swept alley to the pillared portico dimly seen beyond. Not a soul was in sight. The water was already on a level with the banquette, and would soon be running across and into the gate. A vagabond dog skulking about the place gave vent to a mournful howl. A sudden thought struck the captain. He led the way down the slope and forded across to the north side, the others following.

"Joyce," said he to his orderly, "dismount and go in there and ring at the door. Ask if Mr. Lascelles is home. If not, ask if Madame has any message she would like to send to town, or if we can be of any service."

The soldier was gone but a moment, and came hurrying back, a negro boy, holding a long fold of matting over his head to shed the rain, chasing at his heels. It was Alphonse.

"M'sieu' not yet of return," said he, in labored translation of his negro French, "and Madame remain chez Madame d'Hervilly. I am alone wiz my mudder, and she has fear."

"Oh, it's all right, I fancy," said Cram, reassuringly. "They were caught by the storm, and wisely stayed up-town. I saw your gate open, so we stopped to inquire. We'll ride over to Madame d'Hervilly's and ask for them. How came your gate open?"

"*Mo connais pas;* I dunno, sare. It was lock' last night."

"Why, that's odd," said Cram. "Better bolt it now, or all the cattle along the levee will be in there. You can't lock out the water, though. Who had the key besides Mr. Lascelles or Madame?"

"Nobody, sare; but there is muddy foots all over the piazza."

"The devil! I'll have to look in for a moment."

A nod to Pierce brought him too from the

saddle, and the officers handed their reins to the orderlies. Then together they entered the gate and strode up the white shell walk, looking curiously about them through the dripping shrubbery. Again that dismal howl was raised, and Pierce, stopping with impatient exclamation, tore half a brick from the yielding border of the walk and sent it hurtling through the trees. With his tail between his legs, the brute darted from behind a sheltering bush, scurried away around the corner of the house, glancing fearfully back, then, halting at safe distance, squatted on his haunches and lifted up his mournful voice again.

"Whose dog is that?" demanded Cram.

"M'sieu' Philippe's: he not now here. He is de brudder to Monsieur."

At the steps the captain bent and closely examined them and the floor of the low veranda to which they led. Both were disfigured with muddy footprints. Pierce would have gone still further in the investigation, but his senior held up a warning hand.

"Two men have been here," he muttered. "They have tried the door and tried the blinds. —Where did you sleep last night, boy?" and

with the words he turned suddenly on the negro.
" Did you hear no sound ?"

" No, sare. I sleep in my bed,—'way back.
No, I hear noting,—noting." And now the
negro's face was twitching, his eyes staring.
Something in the soldier's stern voice told him
that there was tragedy in the air.

" If this door is locked, go round and open
it from within," said Cram, briefly. Then, as
Alphonse disappeared around the north side, he
stepped back to the shell walk and followed one
of its branches around the other. An instant
later Pierce heard him call. Hastening in his
wake, the youngster came upon his captain
standing under a window, one of whose blinds
was hanging partly open, water standing in pools
all around him.

" Look here," was all he said, and pointed
upward.

The sill was above the level of their heads,
but both could see that the sash was raised.
All was darkness within.

" Come with me," was Cram's next order, and
the lieutenant followed. Alphonse was unlock-
ing the front door, and now threw it open.
Cram strode into the wide hall-way straight to a

door of the east side. It was locked. "Open this, Alphonse," he said.

"I have not the key. It is ever with M'sieu' Lascelles. It is his library."

Cram stepped back, gave one vigorous kick with a heavy riding-boot, and the frail door flew open with a crash. For a moment the darkness was such that no object could be distinguished within. The negro servant hung back, trembling from some indefinable dread. The captain, his hand on the door-knob, stepped quickly into the gloomy apartment, Pierce close at his heels. A broad, flat-topped desk stood in the centre of the room. Some shelves and books were dimly visible against the wall. Some of the drawers of the desk were open, and there was a litter of papers on the desk, and others were strown in the big rattan chair, some on the floor. Two student-lamps could be dimly distinguished, one on the big desk, another on a little reading-table placed not far from the south window, whose blinds, half open, admitted almost the only light that entered the room. With its head near this reading-table and faintly visible, a bamboo lounge stretched its length towards the southward windows, where all was darkness, and something vague and indistinguishable lay extended upon the lounge. Cram marched half-way across the floor, then stopped short, glanced down, and stepped quickly to one side, shifting his heavily-booted feet as though to avoid some such muddy pool as those encountered without.

"Take care," he whispered, and motioned warningly to Pierce. "Come here and open these shutters, Alphonse," were the next words. But once again that prolonged, dismal, mournful howl was heard under the south window, and the negro, seized with uncontrollable panic, turned back and clung trembling to the opposite wall.

"Send one of the men for the post surgeon at once, then come back here," said the captain, and Pierce hastened to the gate. As he returned, the west shutters were being thrown open. There was light when he re-entered the room, and this was what he saw. On the China matting, running from underneath the sofa, fed by heavy drops from above, a dark wet stain. On the lounge, stretched at full length, a stiffening human shape, a yellow-white, parchment-like face above the black clothing, a bluish, half-opened mouth whose yellow teeth showed savagely, a fallen chin and jaw, covered with the gray stubble of unshaved beard, and two staring, sightless, ghastly eyes fixed and upturned as though in agonized appeal. Stone-dead,—murdered, doubtless,—all that was left of the little Frenchman Lascelles.

CHAPTER V.

ALL that day the storm raged in fury; the levee road was blocked in places by the boughs torn from overhanging trees, and here, there, and everywhere turned into a quagmire by the torrents that could find no adequate egress to the northward swamps. For over a mile above the barracks it looked like one vast canal, and by nine o'clock it was utterly impassable. No cars were running on the dilapidated road to the "half-way house," whatever they might be doing beyond. There was only one means of communication between the garrison and the town, and that, on horseback along the crest of the levee, and people in the second-story windows of the store- and dwelling-houses along the other side of the way, driven aloft by the drenched condition of the ground floor, were surprised to see the number of times some Yankee soldier or other made the dismal trip. Cram, with a party of four, was perhaps the first. Before the drip-

ping sentries of the old guard were relieved at
nine o'clock every man and woman at the barracks was aware that foul murder had been done
during the night, and that old Lascelles, slain
by some unknown hand, slashed and hacked in
a dozen places, according to the stories afloat,
lay in his gloomy old library up the levee road,
with a flood already a foot deep wiping out from
the grounds about the house all traces of his
assailants. Dr. Denslow, in examining the body,
found just one deep, downward stab, entering
above the upper rib and doubtless reaching the
heart,—a stab made by a long, straight, sharp,
two-edged blade. He had been dead evidently
some hours when discovered by Cram, who had
now gone to town to warn the authorities, old
Brax meantime having taken upon himself the
responsibility of placing a guard at the house,
with orders to keep Alphonse and his mother in
and everybody else out.

It is hardly worth while to waste time on the
various theories advanced in the garrison as to
the cause and means of the dreadful climax.
That Doyle should be away from the post
provoked neither comment nor speculation: he
was not connected in any way with the tragedy.

But the fact that Mr. Waring was absent all
night, coupled with the stories of his devotions
to Madame, was to several minds *prima facie*
evidence that his was the bloody hand that
wrought the deed,—that he was now a fugitive
from justice, and Madame Lascelles, beyond
doubt, the guilty partner of his flight. Everybody knew by this time of their being together
much of the morning: how could people help
knowing, when Dryden had seen them? In his
elegantly jocular way, Dryden was already con-
doling with Ferry on the probable loss of his
Hatfield clothes, and comforting him with the
assurance that they always gave a feller a new
black suit to be hanged in, so he might get his
duds back after all, only they must get Waring
first. Jeffers doubtless would have been besieged
with questions but for Cram's foresight: his master had ordered him to accompany him to town.

In silence a second time the little party rode
away, passing the flooded homestead where lay
the murdered man, then, farther on, gazing in
mute curiosity at the closed shutters of the
premises some infantry satirists had already
christened "the dove-cot." What cared they
for him or his objectionable helpmate? Still,

they could not but note how gloomy and deserted it all appeared, with two feet of water lapping the garden wall. Summoned by his master, Jeffers knuckled his oil-skin hat-brim and pointed out the spot where Mr. Waring stood when he knocked the cabman into the mud, but Jeffers's tongue was tied and his cockney volubility gone. The tracks made by Cram's wagon up the slope were already washed out. Bending forward to dodge the blinding storm, the party pushed along the embankment until at last the avenues and alleys to their right gave proof of better drainage. At Rampart Street they separated, Pierce going on to report the tragedy to the police, Cram turning to his right and following the broad thoroughfare another mile, until Jeffers, indicating a big, old-fashioned, broad-galleried Southern house standing in the midst of grounds once trim and handsome, but now showing signs of neglect and penury, simply said, " 'Ere, sir." And here the party dismounted.

Cram entered the gate and pulled a clanging bell. The door was almost instantly opened by a colored girl, at whose side, with eager joyous face, was the pretty child he had seen so often playing about the Lascelles homestead, and the eager joyous look faded instantly away.

"She t'ink it M'sieur Vareeng who comes to arrive," explained the smiling colored girl.

"Ah! It is Madame d'Hervilly I wish to see," answered Cram, briefly. "Please take her my card." And, throwing off his dripping rain-coat and tossing it to Jeffers, who had followed to the veranda, the captain stepped within the hall and held forth his hands to Nin Nin, begging her to come to him who was so good a friend of Mr. Waring. But she would not. The tears of disappointment were in the dark eyes as the little one turned and ran away. Cram could hear the gentle, soothing tones of the mother striving to console her child,—the one widowed and the other orphaned by the tidings he bore. Even then he noted how musical, how full of rich melody, was that soft Creole voice. And then Madame d'Hervilly appeared, a stately, dignified, picturesque gentle-woman of perhaps fifty years. She greeted him with punctilious civility, but with manner as distant as her words were few.

"I have come on a trying errand," he began, when she held up a slender, jewelled hand.

" *Pardon. Permettez.*—Madame Lascelles," she
called, and before Cram could find words to
interpose, a servant was speeding to summon
the very woman he had hoped not to have to
see.

" Oh, madame," he murmured low, hurriedly,
" I deplore my ignorance. I cannot speak
French. Try to understand me. Mr. Lascelles
is home, dangerously stricken. I fear the worst.
You must tell her."

" 'Ome! *Là bas? C'est impossible.*"

" It is true," he burst in, for the swish of
silken skirt was heard down the long passage.
"*Il est mort,—mort,*" he whispered, mustering up
what little French he knew and then cursing
himself for an imbecile.

" *Mort! O ciel!*" The words came with a
shriek of anguish from the lips of the elder
woman and were echoed by a scream from beyond. In an instant, wild-eyed, horror-stricken,
Emilie Lascelles had sprung to her tottering
mother's side.

" When? What mean you?" she gasped.

" Madame Lascelles," he sadly spoke, " I had
hoped to spare you this, but it is too late now.
Mr. Lascelles was found lying on the sofa in his

library this morning. He had died hours before, during the night."

And then he had to spring and catch the
fainting woman in his arms. She was still
moaning, and only semi-conscious, when the old
family doctor and her brother, Pierre d'Hervilly,
arrived.

Half an hour later Cram astonished the aides-
de-camp and other bored staff officials by ap-
pearing at the general loafing-room at head-
quarters. To the chorus of inquiry as to what
brought him up in such a storm he made brief
reply, and then asked immediately to speak with
the adjutant-general and Lieutenant Reynolds,
and, to the disgust and mystification of all the
others, he disappeared with these into an adjoining room. There he briefly told the former of
the murder, and then asked for a word with the
junior.

Reynolds was a character. Tall, handsome,
and distinguished, he had served throughout the
war as a volunteer, doing no end of good work,
and getting many a word of praise, but, as all
his service was as a staff officer, it was his
general who reaped the reward of his labors.
He had risen, of course, to the rank of major in

the staff in the volunteers, and everybody had prophesied that he would be appointed a major in the adjutant- or inspector-general's department in the permanent establishment. But there were not enough places by any means, and the few vacancies went to men who knew better how to work for themselves. "Take a lieutenancy now, and we will fix you by and by," was the suggestion, and so it resulted that here he was three years after the war wearing the modest strap of a second lieutenant, doing the duties and accepting the responsibilities of a far higher grade, and being patronized by seniors who were as much his inferiors in rank as they were in ability during the war days. Everybody said it was a shame, and nobody helped to better his lot. He was a man whose counsel was valuable on all manner of subjects. Among other things, he was well versed in all that pertained to the code of honor as it existed in the antebellum days,—had himself been "out," and, as was well known, had but recently officiated as second for an officer who had need of his services. He and Waring were friends from the start, and Cram counted on tidings of his absent subaltern in appealing to him. Great, therefore, was his consternation when in reply to his inquiry Reynolds promptly answered that he had neither seen nor heard from Waring in over forty-eight hours. This was a facer.

"What's wrong, Cram?"

"Read that," said the captain, placing a daintily-written note in the aide-de-camp's hand. It was brief, but explicit:

"COLONEL BRAXTON: Twice have I warned you that the attentions of your Lieutenant Waring to Madame Lascelles meant mischief. This morning, under pretence of visiting her mother, she left the house in a cab, but in half an hour was seen driving with Mr. Waring. This has been, as I have reason to know, promptly carried to Monsieur Lascelles by people whom he had employed for the purpose. I could of told you last night that Monsieur Lascelles's friend had notified Lieutenant Waring that a duel would be exacted should he be seen with Madame again, and now it will certainly come. You have seen fit to scorn my warnings hitherto, the result is on your head." There was no signature whatever.

"Who wrote this rot?" asked Reynolds. "It seems to me I've seen that hand before."

"So have I, and pitched the trash into the fire, as I do everything anonymous that comes my way. But Brax says that this is the second or third, and he's worried about it, and thinks there may be truth in the story."

"As to the duel, or as to the devotions to Madame?" asked Reynolds, calmly.

"We-ll, both, and we thought you would be most apt to know whether a fight was on. Waring promised to return to the post at taps last night. Instead of that, he is gone,—God knows where,—and the old man, the reputed challenger, lies dead at his home. Isn't that ugly?"

Reynolds's face grew very grave.

"Who last saw Waring, that you know of?"

"My man Jeffers left him on Canal Street just after dark last night. He was then going to dine with friends at the St. Charles."

"The Allertons?"

"Yes."

"Then wait till I see the chief, and I'll go with you. Say nothing about this matter yet."

Reynolds was gone but a moment. A little later Cram and the aide were at the St. Charles rotunda, their cards sent up to the Allertons' rooms. Presently down came the bell-boy.

Would the gentleman walk up to the parlor?
This was awkward. They wanted to see Allerton himself, and Cram felt morally confident
that Miss Flora Gwendolen would be on hand
to welcome and chat with so distinguished a
looking fellow as Reynolds. There was no help
for it, however. It would be possible to draw
off the head of the family after a brief call
upon the ladies. Just as they were leaving the
marble-floored rotunda, a short, swarthy man in
"pepper-and-salt" business suit touched Cram
on the arm, begged a word, and handed him a
card.

"A detective,—already?" asked Cram, in
surprise.

"I was with the chief when Lieutenant Pierce
came in to report the matter," was the brief response, "and I came here to see your man. He
is reluctant to tell what he knows without your
consent. Could you have him leave the horses
with your orderly below and come up here a
moment?"

"Why, certainly, if you wish; but I can't see
why," said Cram, surprised.

"You will see, sir, in a moment."

And then Jeffers, with white, troubled face,

11*

appeared, and twisted his wet hat-brim in nervous worriment.

"Now what do you want of him?" asked Cram.

"Ask him, sir, who was the man who slipped a greenback into his hand at the ladies' entrance last evening. What did he want of him?"

Jeffers turned a greenish yellow. His every impulse was to lie, and the detective saw it.

"You need not lie, Jeffers," he said, very quietly. "It will do no good. I saw the men. I can tell your master who one of them was, and possibly lay my hands on the second when he is wanted; but I want you to tell and to explain what that greenback meant."

Then Jeffers broke down and merely blubbered.

"Hi meant no 'arm, sir. Hi never dreamed there was hanythink wrong. 'Twas Mr. Lascelles, sir. 'E said 'e came to thank me for 'elping 'is lady, sir. Then 'e wanted to see Mr. Warink, sir."

"Why didn't you tell me of this before?" demanded the captain, sternly. "You know what happened this morning."

"Hi didn't want to 'ave Mr. Warink suspected,

sir," was poor Jeffers's half-tearful explanation, as Mr. Allerton suddenly entered the little hall-way room.

The grave, troubled faces caught his eye at once.

"Is anything wrong?" he inquired, anxiously. "I hope Waring is all right. I tried to induce him not to start, but he said he had promised and must go."

"What time did he leave you, Mr. Allerton?" asked Cram, controlling as much as possible the tremor of his voice.

"Soon after the storm broke,—about nine-thirty, I should say. He tried to get a cab earlier, but the drivers wouldn't agree to go down for anything less than a small fortune. Luckily, his Creole friends had a carriage."

"His what?"

"His friends from near the barracks. They were here when we came down into the rotunda to smoke after dinner."

Cram felt his legs and feet grow cold and a chill run up his spine.

"Who were they? Did you catch their names?"

"Only one. I was introduced only as they

were about to drive away. A little old fellow
with elaborate manners,—a Monsieur Lascelles."

"And Waring drove away with him?"

"Yes, with him and one other. Seemed to
be a friend of Lascelles. Drove off in a closed
carriage with a driver all done up in rubber and
oil-skin who said he perfectly knew the road.
Why, what's gone amiss?"

CHAPTER VI.

AND all day long the storm beat upon the substantial buildings of the old barracks and flooded the low ground about the sheds and stables. Drills for the infantry were necessarily suspended, several sentries, even, being taken off their posts. The men clustered in the squad-rooms and listened with more or less credulity to the theories and confirmatory statements of fact as related by the imaginative or loquacious of their number. The majority of the officers gathered under the flaring lamp-lights at the sutler's store and occupied themselves pretty much as did their inferiors in grade, though poker and punch—specialties of Mr. Finkbein, the sutler—lent additional color to the stories in circulation.

From this congress the better element of the commissioned force was absent, the names, nationalities, and idiomatic peculiarities of speech of the individual members being iden-

i

tical in most instances with those of their comrades in arms in the ranks. "Brax" had
summoned Minor, Lawrence, Kinsey, and Dryden to hear what the post surgeon had to say on
his return, but cautioned them to keep quiet.
As a result of this precaution, the mystery of
the situation became redoubled by one o'clock,
and was intensified by two, when it was announced that Private Dawson had attempted to
break away out of the hospital after a visit from
the same doctor in his professional capacity.
People were tempted out on their galleries in
the driving storm, and colored servants flitted
from kitchen to kitchen to gather or dispense
new rumors, but nobody knew what to make of
it when, soon after two, an orderly rode in from
town dripping with mud and wet, delivered a
note to the colonel, and took one from him to
Mr. Ferry, now sole representative of the officers of Battery "X" present for duty. Ferry
in return sent the bedraggled horseman on to
the battery quarters with an order to the first
sergeant, and in about fifteen minutes a sergeant
and two men, mounted and each leading a spare
horse, appeared under Ferry's gallery, and that
officer proceeded to occupy one of the vacant

saddles, and, followed by his party, went clattering out of the sally-port and splashing over to
the levee. Stable-call sounded as usual at four
o'clock, and, for the first time in the record of
that disciplined organization since the devas-
tating hand of Yellow Jack was laid upon it the
previous year, no officer appeared to supervise
the grooming and feeding. Two of them were
at the post, however. Mr. Doyle, in arrest on
charge of absence without leave, was escorted to
his quarters about four-fifteen, and was promptly
visited by sympathizing and inquisitive comrades from the Hotel Finkbein, while Mr. Ferry,
who had effected the arrest, was detained
making his report to the post commander.
Night came on apace, the wind began to die
away with the going down of the sun, the rain
ceased to fall, a pallid moon began peering at
odd intervals through rifts in the cloudy veil,
when Cram rode splashing into barracks, worn
with anxiety and care, at eleven o'clock, and,
stopping only for a moment to take his wife in
his arms and kiss her anxious face and shake his
head in response to her eager query for news of
Waring, he hurried down-stairs again and over
to Doyle's quarters. All was darkness there,

but he never hesitated. Tramping loudly over the gallery, he banged at the door, then, turning the knob, intending to burst right in, as was the way in the rough old days, was surprised to find the bolt set.

"Doyle, open. I want to see you at once."

All silence within.

"Doyle, open, or, if you are too drunk to get up, I'll kick in the door."

A groan, a whispered colloquy, then the rattle of bolt and chain. The door opened about an inch, and an oily Irish voice inquired,—

"Hwat's wanted, capt'in?"

"You here?" exclaimed Cram, in disgust. "What business have you in this garrison? If the colonel knew it, you'd be driven out at the point of the bayonet."

"Sure where should wife be but at her husband's side whin he's sick and sufferin'? Didn't they root him out of bed and comfort this day and ride him down like a felon in all the storm? Sure it was the doughboys' orders, sir. I told Doyle the capt'in niver would have——"

"Oh, be quiet: I must see Doyle, and at once."

"Sure he's not able, capt'in. You know how

it is wid him: he's that sinsitive he couldn't bear to talk of the disgrace he's bringin' on the capt'in and the batthery, and I knowed he'd been dhrinkin', sir, and I came back to look for him, but he'd got started, capt'in, and it's——"

"Stop this talk! He wasn't drinking at all until you came back here to hound him. Open that door, or a file of the guard will."

"Och! thin wait till I'm dressed, fur da-cency's sake, capt'in. Sure I'll thry and wake him."

And then more whispering, the clink of glass, maudlin protestation in Doyle's thick tones. Cram banged at the door and demanded instant obedience. Admitted at last, he strode to the side of an ordinary hospital cot, over which the mosquito-bar was now ostentatiously drawn, and upon which was stretched the bulky frame of the big Irishman, his red, blear-eyed, bloated face half covered in his arms. The close air reeked with the fumes of whiskey. In her dis-tress lest Jim should take too much, the claim-ant of his name and protection had evidently been sequestrating a large share for herself.

"How on earth did you get here? Your house was flooded all day," angrily asked Cram.

"Sure we made a raft, sir,—'Louette and me, —and poled over to the levee, and I walked every fut of the way down to follow me husband, as I swore I would whin we was married. I'd 'a' come in Anatole's boat, sir, but 'twas gone,—gone since last night. Did ye know that, capt'in?"

A groan and a feverish toss from the occupant of the narrow bed interrupted her.

"Hush, Jim darlin'! Here's the capt'in to see you and tell you he's come back to have you roighted. Sure how could a poor fellow be expected to come home in all that awful storm this mornin', capt'in? 'Tis for not comin' the colonel had him under arrest; but I tell him the capt'in 'll see him through."

But Cram pushed her aside as she still interposed between him and the bed.

"Doyle, look up and answer. Doyle, I say!"

Again vehement protestations, and now an outburst of tears and pleadings, from the woman.

"Oh, he can't understand you, capt'in. Ah, don't be hard on him. Only this mornin' he was sayin' how the capt'in reminded him of the ould foine days whin the officers was all gintlemen and soldiers. He's truer to ye than all the rest of thim, sir. D'ye moind that, capt'in? Ye wouldn't belave it, mabby, but there's them that can tell ye Loot'nant Waring was no friend of yours, sir, and worse than that, if ould Lascelles could spake now—but there's thim left that can, glory be to God!"

"Oh, for God's sake shut up!" spoke Cram, roughly, goaded beyond all patience. "Doyle, answer me!" And he shook him hard. "You were at the Pelican last night, and you saw Mr. Waring and spoke with him. What did he want of you? Where did he go? Who were with him? Was there any quarrel? Answer, I say! Do you know?" But maudlin moaning and incoherencies were all that Cram could extract from the prostrate man. Again the woman interposed, eager, tearful.

"Sure he was there, capt'in, he *was* there; he told me of it whin I fetched him home last night to git him out of the storm and away from that place; but he's too dhrunk now to talk. Sure there was no gittin' down here to barx for anybody. The cabman, sir, said no carriage could make it."

"What cabman? That's one thing I want to know. Who is he? What became of him?"

"Sure and how do I know, sir? He was a quiet, dacent man, sir; the same that Mr. Waring bate so cruel and made Jeffers kick and bate him too. I saw it all."

"And was he at the Pelican last night? I must know."

"Sure he was indade, sir. Doyle said so whin I fetched him home, and though he can't tell you now, sir, he told me thin. They all came down to the Pelican, sir, Waring and Lascelles and the other gintleman, and they had dhrink, and there was trouble between the Frenchman and Waring,—sure you can't blame him, wid his wife goin' on so wid the loot'nant all the last month,—and blows was struck, and Doyle interposed to stop it, sir, loike the gintleman that he is, and the cab-driver took a hand and pitched him out into the mud. Sure he'd been dhrinkin' a little, sir, and was aisy upset, but that's all he knows. The carriage drove away, and there was three of thim, and poor Doyle got caught out there in the mud and in the storm, and 'twas me wint out wid Dawson and another of the byes and fetched him in. And we niver heerd of the murther at all at all, sir, until I came down here to-day, that's God's troot', and he'll tell ye so whin he's sober," she ended, breathless, reckless of her descriptive confusion of Doyle and Divinity.

And still the Irishman lay there, limp, soggy, senseless, and at last, dismayed and disheartened, the captain turned away.

"Promise to sober him up by reveille, and you may stay. But hear this: if he cannot answer for himself by that time, out you go in the battery cart with a policeman to take you to the calaboose." And then he left.

No sooner had his footsteps died away than the woman turned on her patient, now struggling to a sitting posture.

"Lie still, you thafe and cur, and swear you to every word I say, unless you'd hang in his place. Dhrink this, now, and go to slape, and be riddy to tell the story I give ye in the mornin', or may the knife ye drove in that poor mummy's throat come back to cut your coward heart out."

And Doyle, shivering, sobbing, crazed with drink and fear, covered his eyes with his hands and threw himself back on his hot and steaming pillow.

The morning sun rose brilliant and cloudless

as the horses of the battery came forth from the
dark interior of the stable and, after watering at
the long wooden trough on the platform, were
led away by their white-frocked grooms, each
section to its own picket-line. Ferry, supervis-
ing the duty, presently caught sight of the tall
muscular form of his captain coming briskly
around the corner, little Pierce tripping along
by his side. Cram acknowledged the salute of
the battery officer of the day in hurried fashion.

"Good-morning, Ferry," he said. "Tell me,
who were there when you got Doyle away from
that woman yesterday?"

"Only the three, sir,—Mr. and Mrs. Doyle
and the negro girl."

"No sign of anybody else?"

"None, sir. I didn't go in the house at all.
I rode in the gate and called for Doyle to come
out. The woman tried to parley, but I refused
to recognize her at all, and presently Doyle
obeyed without any trouble whatever, though
she kept up a tirade all the time and said he
was too sick to ride, and all that, but he wasn't.
He seemed dazed, but not drunk,—certainly not
sick. He rode all right, only he shivered and
crossed himself and moaned when he passed the

Lascelles place, for that hound pup set up a howl just as we were opposite the gate. He was all trembling when we reached the post, and took a big drink the moment he got to his room."

"Ye-es, he's been drinking ever since. I've just sent the doctor to see him. Let the corporal and one man of the guard go with the ambulance to escort Mrs. Doyle out of the garrison and take her home. She shall not stay."

"Why, she's gone, sir," said Ferry. "The guard told me she went out of the back gate and up the track towards Anatole's—going for all she was worth—just after dawn."

"The mischief she has! What can have started her? Did you see her yourself, Sergeant Bennett?" asked the captain of a stocky little Irish soldier standing at the moment with drawn sabre awaiting opportunity to speak to his commander.

"Yes, sir," and the sabre came flashing up to the present. "She'd wint over to the hospital to get some medicine for the lieutenant just after our bugle sounded first call, and she came runnin' out as I wint to call the officer of the day, sir. She ran back to the lieutenant's quar-

ters ahead of me, and was up only a minute or
two whin down she came again wid some bun-
dles, and away she wint to the north gate, runnin' wild-like.   The steward told me a moment
after of Dawson's escape."

"Dawson! escaped from hospital?"

"Yes, sir.   They thought he was all right last
evening when he was sleeping, and took the
sentry off, and at four this morning he was
gone."

Florency C. Johnson

CHAPTER VII.

FORTY-EIGHT hours had passed, and not a trace had been found of Lieutenant Waring. The civil officers of the law had held grave converse with the seniors on duty at the barracks, and Cram's face was lined with anxiety and trouble. The formal inquest was held as the flood subsided, and the evidence of the post surgeon was most important. About the throat of the murdered man were indubitable marks of violence. The skin was torn as by finger-nails, the flesh bruised and discolored as by fiercely-grasping fingers. But death, said the doctor, was caused by the single stab. Driven downward with savage force, a sharp-pointed, two-edged, straight-bladed knife had pierced the heart, and all was over in an instant. One other wound there was, a slashing cut across the stomach, which had let a large amount of blood, but might possibly not have been mortal. What part the deceased had taken in the struggle could only be conjectured.

A little five-chambered revolver which he habitually carried was found on the floor close at hand. Two charges had been recently fired, for the barrel was black with powder; but no one had heard a shot.

The bar-keeper at the Pelican could throw but little light on the matter. The storm had broken, he said, with sudden fury. The rain dashed in torrents against his western front, and threatened to beat in the windows. He called to the two men who happened to be seated at a table to assist him, and was busy trying to get up the shutters, when Lieutenant Doyle joined them and rendered timely aid. He had frequently seen Doyle before during the previous month. Mrs. Doyle lived in the old Lemaître house in the block below, and he often supplied them with whiskey. They drank nothing but whiskey. As they ran in the side door they were surprised to see the lights of a carriage standing at the edge of the banquette, and the driver begged for shelter for his team, saying some gentlemen had gone inside. The bar-keeper opened a gate, and the driver put his horses under a shed in a paved court in the rear, then came in for a drink. Meantime, said the

bar-keeper, whose name was Bonelli, three gentlemen who were laughing over their escape
from the storm had ordered wine and gone into
a private room, Doyle with them. The only one
he knew was Monsieur Lascelles, though he had
seen one of the others frequently as he rode by,
and knew him to be an officer before Mr. Doyle
slapped him on the back and hailed him as
"Sammy, old buck!" or something like that.
Mr. Doyle had been drinking, and the gentleman whispered to him not to intrude just then,
and evidently wanted to get rid of him, but Mr.
Lascelles, who had ordered the wine, demanded
to be introduced, and would take no denial, and
invited Mr. Doyle to join them, and ordered
more wine. And then Bonelli saw that Lascelles himself was excited by drink,—the first
time he had ever noticed it in the year he had
known him. The third gentleman he had never
seen before, and could only say he was dark and
sallow and did not talk, except to urge the
driver to make haste,—they must go on; but he
spoke in a low tone with Mr. Lascelles as they
went to the room, and presently the rain seemed
to let up a little, though it blew hard, and the
driver went out and looked around and then re-

turned to the private room where the gentlemen were having their wine, and there was some angry talk, and he came out in a few minutes very mad; said he wouldn't be hired to drive that party any farther, or any other party, for that matter; that no carriage could go down the levee; and then he got out his team and drove back to town; and then Bonelli could hear sounds of altercation in the room, and Mr. Doyle's voice, very angry, and the strange gentleman came out, and one of the men who'd been waiting said he had a cab, if that would answer, and he'd fetch it right off, and by the time he got back it was raining hard again, and he took his cab in under the shed where the carriage had been, and a couple of soldiers from the barracks then came in, wet and cold, and begged for a drink, and Bonelli knew one of them, called Dawson, and trusted him, as he often had done before. When Dawson heard Lieutenant Doyle's drunken voice he said there'd be trouble getting him home, and he'd better fetch Mrs. Doyle, and while he was gone Lascelles came out, excited, and threw down a twenty-dollar bill and ordered more Krug and some brandy, and there was still loud talk, and when Bonelli carried in the bottles Doyle was sitting back in a chair, held down by the other officer, who was laughing at him, but nevertheless had a knife in hand,—a long, sharp, two-edged knife,—and Doyle was calling him names, and was very drunk, and soon after they all went out into the rear court, and Doyle made more noise, and the cab drove away around the corner, going down the levee through the pouring rain, one man on the box with the driver. That was the last he saw. Then Mrs. Doyle came in mad, and demanded her husband, and they found him reeling about the dark court, swearing and muttering, and Dawson and she took him off between them. This must have been before eleven o'clock; and that was absolutely all he knew.

Then Mr. Allerton had told his story again, without throwing the faintest light on the proceedings; and the hack-driver was found, and frankly and fully told his: that Lascelles and another gentleman hired him about eight o'clock to drive them down to the former's place, which they said was several squares above the barracks. He said that he would have to charge them eight dollars such a night anywhere below the old cotton-press, where the pavement ended. But then they had delayed starting nearly an hour, and took another gentleman with them, and when driven by the storm to shelter at the Pelican saloon, three squares below where the pavement ended, and he asked for his money, saying he dare go no farther in the darkness and the flood, the Frenchman wouldn't pay, because he hadn't taken them all the way. He pointed out that he had to bring another gentleman and had to wait a long time, and demanded his eight dollars. The other gentleman, whom he found to be one of the officers at the barracks, slipped a bill into his hand and said it was all he had left, and if it wasn't enough he'd pay him the next time he came to town. But the others were very angry, and called him an Irish thief, and then the big soldier in uniform said he wouldn't have a man abused because he was Irish, and Lieutenant Waring, as he understood the name of this other officer to be, told him, the witness, to slip out and say no more, that he'd fix it all right, and that was the last he saw of the party, but he heard loud words and the sound of a scuffle as he drove away.

And Madame d'Hervilly had given her testimony, which, translated, was to this effect. She had known thé deceased these twenty years. He had been in the employ of her lamented husband, who died of the fever in '55, and Monsieur had succeeded to the business, and made money, and owned property in town, besides the old family residence on the levee below. He was wedded to Emilie only a little while before the war, and lived at home all through, but business languished then, they had to contribute much, and his younger brother, Monsieur Philippe, had cost him a great deal. Philippe was an officer in the Zouaves raised in 1861 among the French Creoles, and marched with them to Columbus, and was wounded and came home to be nursed, and Emilie took care of him for weeks and months, and then he went back to the war and fought bravely, and was shot again and brought home, and this time Monsieur Lascelles did not want to have him down at the house; he said it cost too much to get the doctors down there: so he came under Madame's roof, and she was very fond of the boy, and Emilie would come sometimes and play and sing for him. When the war was

over Monsieur Lascelles gave him money to go to
Mexico with Maximilian, and when the French
were recalled many deserted and came over
to New Orleans, and Monsieur Lascelles was
making very little money now, and had sold his
town property, and he borrowed money of her
to help, as he said, Philippe again, who came to
visit him, and he was often worried by Philippe's
letters begging for money. Seven thousand
dollars now he owed her, and only last week had
asked for more. Philippe was in Key West to
buy an interest in some cigar-business. Monsieur Lascelles said if he could raise three
thousand to reach Philippe this week they
would all make money, but Emilie begged her
not to, she was afraid it would all go, and on
the very day before he was found dead he came
to see her in the afternoon on Rampart Street,
and Emilie had told her of Mr. Waring's kind-
ness to her and to Nin Nin, and how she never
could have got up after being dragged into the
mud by that drunken cabman, "and she begged
me to explain the matter to her husband, who
was a little vexed with her because of Mr. Waring." But he spoke only about the money, and
did not reply about Mr. Waring, except that he

would see him and make proper acknowledg-
ment of his civility. He seemed to think only
of the money, and said Philippe had written
again and must have help, and he was angry at
Emilie because she would not urge with him,
and Emilie wept, and he went away in anger,
saying he had business to detain him in town
until morning, when he would expect her to be
ready to return with him.

Much of this testimony was evoked by
pointed queries of the officials, who seemed
somewhat familiar with Lascelles's business and
family affairs, and who then declared that they
must question the stricken widow. Harsh and
unfeeling as this may have seemed, there were
probably reasons which atoned for it. She came
in on the arm of the old family physician, looking like a drooping flower, with little Nin Nin
clinging to her hand. She was so shocked and
stunned that she could barely answer the questions put to her with all courtesy and gentle-
ness of manner. No, she had never heard of
any quarrel between Monsieur Lascelles and his
younger brother. Yes, Philippe had been nursed
by her through his wounds. She was fond of
Philippe, but not so fond as was her husband.

13*

Mr. Lascelles would do anything for Philippe, deny himself anything almost. Asked if Monsieur Lascelles had not given some reason for his objection to Philippe's being nursed at his house when he came home the second time, she was embarrassed and distressed. She said Philippe was an impulsive boy, fancied himself in love with his brother's wife, and Armand saw something of this, and at last upbraided him, but very gently. There was no quarrel at all. Was there any one whom Monsieur Lascelles had been angered with on her account? She knew of none, but blushed, and blushed painfully. Had the deceased not recently objected to the attentions paid her by other gentlemen? There was a murmur of reproach among the hearers, but Madame answered unflinchingly, though with painful blushes and tears. Monsieur Lascelles had said nothing of disapproval until very recently; *au contraire*, he had much liked Mr. Waring. He was the only one of the officers at the barracks whom he had ever invited to the house, and he talked with him a great deal; had never, even to her, spoken of a quarrel with him because Mr. Waring had been so polite to her, until within a week or two; then—yes, he certainly had. Of her husband's business affairs, his papers, etc., she knew little. He always had certain moneys, though not large sums, with all his papers, in the drawers of his cabinet, and that they should be in so disturbed a state was not unusual. They were all in order, closed and locked, when he started for town the morning of that fatal day, but he often left them open and in disorder, only then locking his library door. When she left for town, two hours after him, the library door was open, also the side window. She could throw no light on the tragedy. She had no idea who the stranger could be. She had not seen Philippe for nearly a year, and believed him to be at Key West.

Alphonse, the colored boy, was so terrified by the tragedy and by his detention under the same roof with the murdered man that his evidence was only dragged from him. Nobody suspected the poor fellow of complicity in the crime, yet he seemed to consider himself as on trial. He swore he had entered the library only once during the afternoon or evening, and that was to close the shutters when the storm broke. He left a lamp burning low in the hall, according to custom, though he felt sure his master and mistress would remain in town over-night rather than attempt to come down. He had slept soundly, as negroes will, despite the gale and the roar of the rain that drowned all other noises. It was late the next morning when his mother called him. The old mammy was frightened to see the front gate open, the deep water in the streets, and the muddy footprints on the veranda. She called Alphonse, who found that his master must have come in during the night, after all, for the lamp was taken from the hall table, the library door was closed and locked, so was the front door, also barred within, which it had not been when he went to bed. He tapped at the library, got no answer, so tip-toed to his master's bedroom; it was empty and undisturbed. Neither had Madame nor Made-moiselle Nin Nin been to their rooms. Then he was troubled, and then the soldiers came and called him out into the rain. They could tell the rest.

Cram's story is already told, and he could add nothing. The officials tried to draw the battery-man out as to the relations existing between Lieutenant Waring and Madame, but got badly "bluffed." Cram said he had never seen anything in the faintest degree worthy of comment. Had he heard anything? Yes, but nothing worthy of consideration, much less of repetition. Had he not loaned Mr. Waring his team and carriage to drive Madame to town that morning? No. How did he get it, then? Took it! Was Monsieur Waring in the habit of helping himself to the property of his brother officers? Yes, whenever he felt like it, for they never objected. The legal official thought such spirit of *camaraderie* in the light artillery must make life at the barracks something almost poetic, to which Cram responded, "Oh, at times absolutely idyllic." And the tilt ended with the civil functionary ruffled, and this was bad for the battery. Cram never had any policy whatsoever.

Lieutenant Doyle was the next witness summoned, and a more God-forsaken-looking fellow never sat in a shell jacket. Still in arrest, physically, at the beck of old Braxton, and similarly hampered, intellectually, at the will of bold John Barleycorn, Mr. Doyle came before the civil authorities only upon formal subpœna served at post head-quarters. The post surgeon had straightened him up during the day, but was utterly perplexed at his condition. Mrs.

Doyle's appearance in the neighborhood some
weeks before had been the signal for a series of
sprees on the Irishman's part that had on two
occasions so prostrated him that Dr. Potts, an
acting assistant surgeon, had been called in to
prescribe for him, and, thanks to the vigorous
constitution of his patient, had pulled him out
in a few hours.   But this time " Pills the Less"
had found Doyle in a state bordering on terror,
even when assured that the quantity of his pota-
tions had not warranted an approach to tremens.
The post surgeon had been called in too, and
" Pills the Pitiless," as he was termed, thanks to
his unfailing prescription of quinine and blue
mass in the shape and size of buckshot, having
no previous acquaintance, in Doyle, with these
attacks, poohpoohed the case, administered bro-
mides and admonition in due proportion, and
went off about more important business.   Dr.
Potts, however, stood by his big patient, wondering what should cause him to start in such
terror at every step upon the stair without, and
striving to bring sleep to eyes that had not
closed the livelong night nor all the balmy,
beautiful day.   Once he asked if Doyle wished
him to send for his wife, and was startled at the

vehemei.ce of the reply, "For God's sake, no!" and, shuddering, Doyle had hidden his face and turned away. Potts got him to eat something towards noon, and Doyle begged for more drink, but was refused. He was sober, yet shattered, when Mr. Drake suddenly appeared just about stable-call and bade him repair at once to the presence of the commanding officer. Then Potts *had* to give him a drink, or he would never have got there. With the aid of a servant he was dressed, and, accompanied by the doctor, reached the office. Braxton looked him over coldly.

"Mr. Doyle," said he, "the civil authorities have made requisition for——" But he had got no further when Doyle staggered, and but for the doctor's help might have fallen.

"For God's sake, colonel, it isn't true! Sure I know nothing of it at all at all, sir. Indade, indade, I was blind dhrunk, colonel. Sure they'd swear a man's life away, sir, just because he was the one—he was the one that——"

"Be silent, sir. You are not accused, that I know of. It is as a witness you are needed.— Is he in condition to testify, doctor?"

"He is well enough, sir, to tell what he

knows, but he claims to know nothing." And this, too, Doyle eagerly seconded, but was sent along in the ambulance, with the doctor to keep him out of mischief, and a parting shot to the effect that when the coroner was through with him the post commander would take hold again, so the colonel depressed more than the cocktail stimulated, and, as luck would have it, almost the first person to meet him inside the gloomy enclosure was his wife, and her few whispered words only added to his misery.

The water still lay in pools about the premises, and the police had allowed certain of the neighbors to stream in and stare at the white walls and shaded windows, but only a favored few penetrated the hall-way and rooms where the investigation was being held. Doyle shook like one with the palsy as he ascended the little flight of steps and passed into the open door-way, still accompanied by "Little Pills." People looked at him with marked curiosity. He was questioned, re-questioned, cross-questioned, but the result was only a hopeless tangle. He really added nothing to the testimony of the hack-driver and Bonelli. In abject remorse and misery he begged them to understand he was

drunk when he joined the party, got drunker,
dimly remembered there was a quarrel, but he
had no cause to quarrel with any one, and that
was all; he never knew how he got home. He
covered his face in his shaking hands at last,
and seemed on the verge of a fit of crying.

But then came sensation.

Quietly rising from his seat, the official who
so recently had had the verbal tilt with Cram
held forth a rusty, cross-hilted, two-edged knife
that looked as though it might have lain in the
mud and wet for hours.

"Have you ever seen this knife before?" he
asked. And Doyle, lifting up his eyes one instant, groaned, shuddered, and said,—

"Oh, my God, yes!"

"Whose property is it or was it?"

At first he would not reply. He moaned and
shook. At last—

"Sure the initials are on the top," he cried.

But the official was relentless.

"Tell us what they are and what they
represent."

People were crowding the hall-way and forcing
themselves into the room. Cram and Ferry,
curiously watching their ill-starred comrade,

14

had exchanged glances of dismay when the knife was so suddenly produced. Now they bent breathlessly forward.

The silence for the moment was oppressive.

"If it's the knife I mane," he sobbed at last, desperately, miserably, "the letters are S. B. W., and it belongs to Lieutenant Waring of our bathery."

But no questioning, however adroit, could elicit from him the faintest information as to how it got there. The last time he remembered seeing it, he said, was on Mr. Waring's table the morning of the review. A detective testified to having found it among the bushes under the window as the water receded. Ferry and the miserable Ananias were called, and they, too, had to identify the knife, and admit that neither had seen it about the room since Mr. Waring left for town. Of other witnesses called, came first the proprietor of the stable to which the cab belonged. Horse and cab, he said, covered with mud, were found under a shed two blocks below the French Market, and the only thing in the cab was a handsome silk umbrella, London make, which Lieutenant Pierce laid claim to. Mrs. Doyle swore that as she was going in search of her husband she met the cab just below the Pelican, driving furiously away, and that in the flash of lightning she recognized the driver as the man whom Lieutenant Waring had beaten that morning on the levee in front of her place. A stranger was seated beside him. There were two gentlemen inside, but she saw the face of only one,— Lieutenant Waring.

Nobody else could throw any light on the matter. The doctor, recalled, declared the knife or dagger was shaped exactly as would have to be the one that gave the death-blow. Everything pointed to the fact that there had been a struggle, a deadly encounter, and that after the fatal work was done the murderer or murderers had left the doors locked and barred and escaped through the window, leaving the desk rifled and carrying away what money there was, possibly to convey the idea that it was only a vulgar murder and robbery, after all.

Of other persons who might throw light upon the tragedy the following were missing: Lieutenant Waring, Private Dawson, the cabman, and the unrecognized stranger. So, too, was Anatole's boat.

CHAPTER VIII.

WHEN four days and nights had passed away without a word or sign from Waring, the garrison had come to the conclusion that those officers or men of Battery "X" who still believed him innocent were idiots. So did the civil authorities; but those were days when the authorities of Louisiana commanded less respect from its educated people than did even the military. The police force, like the State, was undergoing a process called reconstruction, which might have been impressive in theory, but was ridiculous in practice. A reward had been offered by business associates of the deceased for the capture and conviction of the assassin. A distant relative of old Lascelles had come to take charge of the place until Monsieur Philippe should arrive. The latter's address had been found among old Armand's papers, and despatches, *via* Havana, had been sent to him, also letters. Pierre d'Hervilly had taken the weeping widow and little Nin Nin to *bonne maman's* to stay. Alphonse and his woolly-pated mother, true to negro superstitions, had decamped. Nothing would induce them to remain under the roof where foul murder had been done. "De hahnts" was what they were afraid of. And so the old white homestead, though surrounded on every side by curiosity-seekers and prying eyes, was practically deserted. Cram went about his duties with a heavy heart and light aid. Ferry and Pierce both commanded sections now, as Doyle remained in close arrest and "Pills the Less" in close attendance. Something was utterly wrong with the fellow. Mrs. Doyle had not again ventured to show her red nose within the limits of the "barx," as she called them, a hint from Braxton having proved sufficient; but that she was ever scouting the pickets no one could doubt. Morn, noon, and night she prowled about the neighborhood, employing the "byes," so she termed such stray sheep in army blue as a dhrop of Anatole's best would tempt, to carry scrawling notes to Jim, one of which, falling with its postman by the wayside and turned over by the guard to Captain Cram for transmittal, was addressed to Mister Loot'nt James Doyle,

Lite Bothery X, Jaxun Barx, and brought the
only laughter to his lips the big horse-artillery-
man had known for nearly a week. Her customary Mercury, Dawson, had vanished from
sight, dropped, with many another and often a
better man, as a deserter.

Over at Waring's abandoned quarters the
shades were drawn and the green *jalousies* bolted.
Pierce stole in each day to see that everything,
even to the augmented heap of letters, was undisturbed, and Ananias drooped in the court
below and refused to be comforted. Cram had
duly notified Waring's relatives, now living in
New York, of his strange and sudden disappearance, but made no mention of the cloud
of suspicion which had surrounded his name.
Meantime, some legal friends of the family were
overhauling the Lascelles papers, and a dark-
complexioned, thick-set, active little civilian was
making frequent trips between department head-
quarters and barracks. At the former he com-
pared notes with Lieutenant Reynolds, and at
the latter with Braxton and Cram. The last
interview Mr. Allerton had before leaving with
his family for the North was with this same
lively party, the detective who joined them that

night at the St. Charles, and Allerton, being a
man of much substance, had tapped his pocket-
book significantly.

"The difficulty just now is in having a talk
with the widow," said this official to Cram and
Reynolds, whom he had met by appointment
on the Thursday following the eventful Saturday of Braxton's "combined" review. "She is
too much prostrated. I've simply got to wait
awhile, and meantime go about this other affair.
Is there no way in which you can see her?"

Cram relapsed into a brown study. Reynolds
was poring over the note written to Braxton
and comparing it with one he held in his hand,
—an old one, and one that told an old, old story.
"I know you'll say I have no right to ask this,"
it read, "but you're a gentleman, and I'm a
friendless woman deserted by a worthless husband. My own people are ruined by the war,
but even if they had money they wouldn't send
any to me, for I offended them all by marrying
a Yankee officer. God knows I am punished
enough for that. But I was so young and
innocent when he courted me. I ought to of
left—I would of left him as soon as I found out
how good-for-nothing he really was, only I was

so much in love I couldn't. I was fastenated, I suppose. Now I've sold everything, but if you'll only lend me fifty dollars I'll work my fingers to the bone until I pay it. For the old home's sake, please do."

"It's the same hand,—the same woman, Cram, beyond a doubt. She bled Waring for the old home's sake the first winter he was in the South. He told me all about it two years ago in Washington, when we heard of her the second time. Now she's followed him over here, or got here first, tried the same game probably, met with a refusal, and this anonymous note is her revenge. The man she married was a crack-brained weakling who got into the army the fag end of the war, fell in love with her pretty face, married her, then they quarrelled, and he drank himself into a muddle-head. She ran him into debt; then he gambled away government funds, bolted, was caught, and would have been tried and sent to jail, but some powerful relative saved him that, and simply had him dropped;—never heard of him again. She was about a month grass-widowed when Waring came on his first duty there. He had an uncongenial lot of brother officers for a two-

company post, and really had known of this girl
and her people before the war, and she appealed
to him, first for sympathy and help, then charity,
then blackmail, I reckon, from which his fever
saved him. Then she struck some quartermaster or other and lived off him for a while;
drifted over here, and no sooner did he arrive,
all ignorant of her presence in or around New
Orleans, than she began pestering him again.
When he turned a deaf ear, she probably threatened, and then came these anonymous missives
to you and Braxton. Yours always came by
mail, you say. The odd thing about the colonel's—this one, at least—is that it was with his
mail, but never came through the post-office."

"That's all very interesting," said the little
civilian, dryly, "but what we want is evidence
to acquit him and convict somebody else of Lascelles's death. What has this to do with the
other?"

"This much: This letter came to Braxton by
hand, not by mail,—by hand, probably direct
from her. What hand had access to the office
the day when the whole command was out at
review? Certainly no outsider. The mail is
opened and distributed on its arrival at nine

o'clock by the chief clerk, or by the sergeant-major, if he happens to be there, though he's generally at guard mount. On this occasion he was out at review. Leary, chief clerk, tells Colonel Braxton he opened and distributed the mail, putting the colonel's on his desk; Root was with him and helped. The third clerk came in later; had been out all night, drinking. His name is Dawson. Dawson goes out again and gets fuller, and when next brought home is put in hospital under a sentry. Then he hears of the murder, bolts, and isn't heard from since, except as the man who helped Mrs. Doyle to get her husband home. *He* is the fellow who brought that note. He knew something of its contents, for the murder terrified him, and he ran away. Find his trail, and you strike that of the woman who wrote these."

"By the Lord, lieutenant, if you'll quit the army and take my place you'll make a name and a fortune."

"And if you'll quit your place and take mine you'll get your *coup de grâce* in some picayune Indian fight and be forgotten. So stay where you are; but find Dawson, find her, find what they know, and you'll be famous."

CHAPTER IX.

THAT night, or very early next morning, there was pandemonium at the barracks. It was clear, still, beautiful. A soft April wind was drifting up from the lower coast, laden with the perfume of sweet olive and orange blossoms. Mrs. Cram, with one or two lady friends and a party of officers, had been chatting in low tone upon their gallery until after eleven, but elsewhere about the moonlit quadrangle all was silence when the second relief was posted. Far at the rear of the walled enclosure, where, in deference to the manners and customs of war as observed in the good old days whereof our seniors tell, the sutler's establishment was planted within easy hailing-distance of the guard-house, there was still the sound of modified revelry by night, and poker and whiskey punch had gathered their devotees in the grimy parlors of Mr. Finkbein, and here the belated ones tarried until long after midnight, as most of them were

bachelors and had no better halves, as had
Doyle, to fetch them home "out of the wet."
Cram and his lieutenants, with the exception
of Doyle, were never known to patronize this
establishment, whatsoever they might do outside. They had separated before midnight, and
little Pierce, after his customary peep into Waring's preserves, had closed the door, gone to
his own room, to bed and to sleep. Ferry, as
battery officer of the day, had made the rounds
of the stables and gun-shed about one o'clock,
and had encountered Captain Kinsey, of the
infantry, coming in from his long tramp through
the dew-wet field, returning from the inspection
of the sentry-post at the big magazine.

"No news of poor Sam yet, I suppose?" said
Kinsey, sadly, as the two came strolling in together through the rear gate.

"Nothing whatever," was Ferry's answer.
"We cannot even form a conjecture, unless he,
too, has been murdered. Think of there being
a warrant out for his arrest,—for him, Sam
Waring!"

"Well," said Kinsey, "no other conclusion
could be well arrived at, unless that poor brute
Doyle did it in a drunken row. Pills says he

never saw a man so terror-stricken as he seems to be. He's afraid to leave him, really, and Doyle's afraid to be alone,—thinks the old woman may get in."

"She has no excuse for coming, captain," said Ferry. "When she told Cram she must see her husband to-day, that she was out of money and starving, the captain surprised her by handing her fifty dollars, which is much more than she'd have got from Doyle. She took it, of course, but that isn't what she wanted. She wants to get at him. She has money enough."

"Yes, that woman's a terror, Ferry. Old Mrs. Murtagh, wife of my quartermaster sergeant, has been in the army twenty years, and says she knew her well,—knew all her people. She comes from a tough lot, and they had a bad reputation in Texas in the old days. Doyle's a totally different man since she turned up, Cram tells me. Hello! here's 'Pills the Less,'" he suddenly exclaimed, as they came opposite the west gate, leading to the hospital. "How's your patient, Doc?"

"Well, he's sleeping at last. He seems worn out. It's the first time I've left him, but I'm

H

used up and want a few hours' sleep. There
isn't anything to drink in the room, even if he
should wake, and Jim is sleeping or lying there
by him."

"Oh, he'll do all right now, I reckon," said
the officer of the day, cheerfully. "Go and get
your sleep. The old woman can't get at him
unless she bribes my sentries or rides the air on
a broomstick, like some other old witches I've
read of. Ferry sleeps in the adjoining room,
anyhow, so he can look out for her. Good-
night, Doc." And so, on they went, glancing
upward at the dim light just showing through
the window-blinds in the gable end of Doyle's
quarters, and halting at the foot of the stairs.

"Come over and have a pipe with me, Ferry,"
said the captain. "It's too beautiful a night to
turn in. I want to talk to you about Waring,
anyhow. This thing weighs on my mind."

"Done with you, for an hour, anyhow!" said
Ferry. "Just wait a minute till I run up and
get my baccy."

Presently down came the young fellow again,
meerschaum in hand, the moonlight glinting on
his slender figure, so trim and jaunty in the
battery dress. Kinsey looked him over with a

smile of soldierly approval and a whimsical comment on the contrast between the appearance of this young artillery sprig and that of his own stout personality, clad as he was in a bulging blue flannel sack-coat, only distinguishable in cut and style from civilian garb by its having brass buttons and a pair of tarnished old shoulder-straps. Ferry was a swell. His shell jacket fitted like wax. The Russian shoulder-knots of twisted gold were of the handsomest make. The riding-breeches, top-boots, and spurs were such that even Waring could not criticise. His sabre gleamed in the moonbeams, and Kinsey's old leather-covered sword looked dingy by contrast. His belt fitted trim and taut, and was polished as his boot-tops; Kinsey's sank down over the left hip, and was worn brown. The sash Ferry sported as battery officer of the day was draped, West Point fashion, over the shoulder and around the waist, and accurately knotted and looped; Kinsey's old war-worn crimson net was slung higgledy-piggledy over his broad chest.

"What swells you fellows are, Ferry!" he said, laughingly, as the youngster came dancing down. "Even old Doyle gets out here in his

scarlet plume occasionally and puts us doughboys to shame. What's the use in trying to
make such a rig as ours look soldierly? If it
were not for the brass buttons our coats would
make us look like parsons and our hats like
monkeys. As for this undress, all that can be
said in its favor is, you can't spoil it even by
sleeping out on the levee in it, as I am sometimes tempted to do. Let's go out there now."

It was perhaps quarter of two when they took
their seats on the wooden bench under the trees,
and, lighting their pipes, gazed out over the
broad sweeping flood of the Mississippi, gleam-
ing like a silvered shield in the moonlight.
Far across at the opposite shore the low line of
orange-groves and plantation houses and quarters was merged in one long streak of gloom,
relieved only at intervals by twinkling light.
Farther up-stream, like dozing sea-dogs, the
fleet of monitors lay moored along the bank,
with the masts and roofs of Algiers dimly out-
lined against the crescent sweep of lights that
marked the levee of the great Southern metropolis, still prostrate from the savage buffeting of
the war, yet so soon to rouse from lethargy, re-
sume her sway, and, stretching forth her arms,

to draw once again to her bosom the wealth and
tribute, tenfold augmented, of the very heart of
the nation, until, mistress of the commerce of a
score of States, she should rival even New York
in the volume of her trade. Below them, away
to the east towards English Turn, rolled the
tawny flood, each ripple and eddy and swirling
pool crested with silver,—the twinkling lights
at Chalmette barely distinguishable from dim,
low-hanging stars. Midway the black hulk of
some big ocean voyager was forging slowly,
steadily towards them, the red light of the port
side already obscured, the white and green
growing with every minute more and more distinct, and, save the faint rustle of the leaves
overhead, murmuring under the touch of the
soft, southerly night wind, the plash of wavelet
against the wooden pier, and the measured foot-
fall of the sentry on the flagstone walk in front
of the sally-port, not a sound was to be heard.

For a while they smoked in silence, enjoying
the beauty of the night, though each was thinking only of the storm that swept over the scene
the Sunday previous and of the tragedy that
was borne upon its wings. At last Kinsey
shook himself together.

"Ferry, sometimes I come out here for a quiet smoke and think. Did it ever occur to you what a fearful force, what illimitable power, there is sweeping by us here night after night with never a sound?"

"Oh, you mean the Mississip," said Ferry, flippantly. "It would be a case of mops and brooms, I fancy, if she were to bust through the bank and sweep us out into the swamps."

"Exactly! that's in case she broke loose, as you say; but even when in the shafts, as she is now, between the levees, how long would it take her to sweep a fellow from here out into the gulf, providing nothing interposed to stop him?"

"Matter of simple mathematical calculation," said Ferry, practically. "They say it's an eight-mile current easy out there in the middle where she's booming. Look at that barrel scooting down yonder. Now, I'd lay a fiver I could cut loose from here at reveille and shoot the passes before taps and never pull a stroke. It's less than eighty miles down to the forts."

"Well, then, a skiff like that that old Anatole's blaspheming about losing wouldn't take very long to ride over that route, would it?" said Kinsey, reflectively.

" No, not if allowed to slide. But somebody'd be sure to put out and haul it in as a prize, —flotsam and what-you-may-call-'em. You see these old niggers all along here with their skiffs tacking on to every bit of drift-wood that's worth having."

".But, Ferry, do you think they'd venture out in such a storm as Sunday last?—think anything could live in it short of a decked ship ?"

" No, probably not. Certainly not Anatole's boat."

" Well, that's just what I'm afraid of, and what Cram and Reynolds dread."

" Do they ? Well, so far as that storm's concerned, it would have blown it down-stream until it came to the big bend below here to the east. Then, by rights, it ought to have blown against the left bank. But every inch of it has been scouted all the way to quarantine. The whole river was filled with drift, though, and it might have been wedged in a lot of logs and swept out anyhow. Splendid ship, that! Who is she, do you suppose ?"

The great black hull with its lofty tracery of masts and spars was now just about opposite the barracks, slowly and majestically ascending **the** stream.

"One of those big British freight steamers that moor there below the French Market, I reckon. They seldom come up at night unless it's in the full of the moon, and even then they move with the utmost caution. See, she's slowing up now."

"Hello! Listen! What's that?" exclaimed Ferry, starting to his feet.

A distant, muffled cry. A distant shot. The sentry at the sally-port dashed through the echoing vault, then bang! came the loud roar of his piece, followed by the yell of—

"Fire! fire! *The guard !*"

With one spring Ferry was down the levee and darted like a deer across the road, Kinsey lumbering heavily after. Even as he sped through the stone-flagged way, the hoarse roar of the drum at the guard-house, followed instantly by the blare of the bugle from the battery quarters, sounded the stirring alarm. A shrill, agonized female voice was madly screaming for help. Guards and sentries were rushing to the scene, and flames were bursting from the front window of Doyle's quarters. Swift though

Ferry ran, others were closer to the spot. Half a dozen active young soldiers, members of the infantry guard, had sprung to the rescue. When Ferry dashed up to the gallery he was just in time to stumble over a writhing and prostrate form, to help extinguish the blazing clothing of another, to seize his water-bucket and douse its contents over a third,—one yelling, the others stupefied by smoke—or something. In less time than it takes to tell it, daring fellows had ripped down the blazing shades and shutters, tossed them to the parade beneath, dumped a heap of soaked and smoking bedding out of the rear windows, splashed a few bucketfuls of water about the recking room, and the fire was out. But the doctors were working their best to bring back the spark of life to two senseless forms, and to still the shrieks of agony that burst from the scared and blistered lips of Bridget Doyle.

While willing hands bore these scorched semblances of humanity to neighboring rooms and tender-hearted women hurried to add their ministering touch, and old Braxton ordered the excited garrison back to quarters and bed, he, with Cram and Kinsey and Ferry, made prompt examination of the premises. On the table two whiskey-bottles, one empty, one nearly full, that Dr. Potts declared were not there when he left at one. On the mantel a phial of chloroform, which was also not there before. But a towel soaked with the stifling contents lay on the floor by Jim's rude pallet, and a handkerchief half soaked, half consumed, was on the chair which had stood by the bedside, among the fragments of an overturned kerosene lamp.

A quick examination of the patients showed that Jim, the negro, had been chloroformed and was not burned at all, that Doyle was severely burned and had probably inhaled flames, and that the woman was crazed with drink, terror, and burns combined. It took the efforts of two or three men and the influence of powerful opiates to quiet her. Taxed with negligence or complicity on the part of the sentry, the sergeant of the guard repudiated the idea, and assured Colonel Braxton that it was an easy matter for any one to get either in or out of the garrison without encountering the sentry, and, taking his lantern, led the way out to the hospital grounds by a winding foot-path among the trees to a point in the high white picket fence where two slats had been shoved aside. Any one coming along the street without could pass far beyond the ken of the sentry at the west gate, and slip in with the utmost ease, and once inside, all that was necessary was to dodge possible reliefs and patrols. No sentry was posted at the gate through the wall that separated the garrison proper from the hospital grounds. Asked why he had not reported this, the sergeant smiled and said there were a dozen others just as convenient, so what was the use? He did not say, however, that he and his fellows had recourse to them night after night.

It was three o'clock when the officers' families fairly got settled down again and back to their beds, and the silence of night once more reigned over Jackson Barracks. One would suppose that such a scene of terror and excitement was enough, and that now the trembling, frightened women might be allowed to sleep in peace; but it was not to be. Hardly had one of their number closed her eyes, hardly had all the flickering lights, save those at the hospital and guardhouse, been downed again, when the strained nerves of the occupants of the officers' quadrangle were jumped into mad jangling once

more and all the barracks aroused a second
time, and this, too, by a woman's shriek of
horror.

Mrs. Conroy, a delicate, fragile little body,
wife of a junior lieutenant of infantry occupy-
ing a set of quarters in the same building with,
but at the opposite end from, Pierce and Waring, was found lying senseless at the head of
the gallery stairs.

When revived, amid tears and tremblings and
incoherent exclamations she declared that she
had gone down to the big ice-chest on the
ground-floor to get some milk for her nervous
and frightened child and was hurrying noiselessly up the stairs again,—the only means of
communication between the first and second
floors,—when, face to face, in front of his door,
she came upon Mr. Waring, or his ghost; that
his eyes were fixed and glassy; that he did not
seem to see her even when he spoke, for speak
he did. His voice sounded like a moan of anguish, she said, but the words were distinct:
"Where is my knife? Who has taken my
knife?"

And then little Pierce, who had helped to
raise and carry the stricken woman to her room,

suddenly darted out on the gallery and ran along to the door he had closed four hours earlier. It was open. Striking a match, he hurried through into the chamber beyond, and there, face downward upon the bed, lay his friend and comrade Waring, moaning like one in the delirium of fever.

CHAPTER X.

LIEUTENANT REYNOLDS was seated at his desk at department head-quarters about nine o'clock that morning when an orderly in light-battery dress dismounted at the banquette and came up the stairs three at a jump. "Captain Cram's compliments, sir, and this is immediate," he reported, as he held forth a note. Reynolds tore it open, read it hastily through, then said, "Go and fetch me a cab quick as you can," and disappeared in the general's room. Half an hour later he was spinning down the levee towards the French Market, and before ten o'clock was seated in the captain's cabin of the big British steamer Ambassador, which had arrived at her moorings during the night. Cram and Kinsey were already there, and to them the skipper was telling his story.

Off the Tortugas, just about as they had shaped their course for the Belize, they were hailed by the little steamer Tampa, bound from

New Orleans to Havana. The sea was calm, and a boat put off from the Tampa and came alongside, and presently a gentleman was assisted aboard. He seemed weak from illness, but explained that he was Lieutenant Waring, of the United States Artillery, had been accidentally carried off to sea, and the Ambassador was the first inward-bound ship they had sighted since crossing the bar. He would be most thankful for a passage back to New Orleans. Captain Baird had welcomed him with the heartiness of the British tar, and made him at home in his cabin. The lieutenant was evidently far from well, and seemed somewhat dazed and mentally distressed. He could give no account of his mishap other than that told him by the officers of the Tampa, which had lain to when overtaken by the gale on Saturday night, and on Sunday morning when they resumed their course down-stream they overhauled a light skiff and were surprised to find a man aboard, drenched and senseless. "The left side of his face was badly bruised and discolored, even when he came to us," said Baird, "and he must have been slugged and robbed, for his watch, his seal-ring, and what little money

he had were all gone." The second officer of
the Tampa had fitted him out with a clean shirt,
and the steward dried his clothing as best he
could, but the coat was stained and clotted with
blood. Mr. Waring had slept heavily much of
the way back until they passed Pilot Town.
Then he was up and dressed Thursday afternoon, and seemingly in better spirits, when he
picked up a copy of the New Orleans *Picayune*
which the pilot had left aboard, and was reading
that, when suddenly he started to his feet with
an exclamation of amaze, and, when the captain
turned to see what was the matter, Waring was
ghastly pale and fearfully excited by something
he had read. He hid the paper under his coat
and sprang up on deck and paced nervously to
and fro for hours, and began to grow so ill,
apparently, that Captain Baird was much worried. At night he begged to be put ashore at
the barracks instead of going on up to town,
and Baird had become so troubled about him
that he sent his second officer in the gig with
him, landed him on the levee opposite the sally-
port, and there, thanking them heartily, but de-
clining further assistance, Waring had hurried
through the entrance into the barrack square.

Mr. Royce, the second officer, said there was considerable excitement, beating of drums and sounding of bugles, at the post, as they rowed towards the shore. He did not learn the cause. Captain Baird was most anxious to learn if the gentleman had safely reached his destination. Cram replied that he had, but in a state bordering on delirium and unable to give any coherent account of himself. He could tell he had been aboard the Ambassador and the Tampa, but that was about all.

And then they told Baird that what Waring probably saw was Wednesday's paper with the details of the inquest on the body of Lascelles and the chain of evidence pointing to himself as the murderer. This caused honest Captain Baird to lay ten to one he wasn't, and five to one he'd never heard of it till he got the paper above Pilot Town. Whereupon all three officers clapped the Briton on the back and shook him by the hand and begged his company to dinner at the barracks and at Moreau's; and then, while Reynolds sped to the police-office and Kinsey back to Colonel Braxton, whom he represented at the interview, Cram re-mounted, and, followed by the faithful Jeffers,

16*

trotted up Rampart Street and sent in his card
to Madame Lascelles, and Madame's maid
brought back reply that she was still too shocked
and stricken to receive visitors. So also did
Madame d'Hervilly deny herself, and Cram rode
home to Nell.

"It is useless," he said. "She will not see
me."

"Then she shall see me," said Mrs. Cram.

And so a second time did Jeffers make the
trip to town that day, this time perched with
folded arms in the rumble of the pony-phaeton.

And while she was gone, the junior doctor
was having the liveliest experience of his few
years of service. Scorched and burned though
she was, Mrs. Doyle's faculties seemed to have
returned with renewed acuteness and force.
She demanded to be taken to her husband's side,
but the doctor sternly refused. She demanded
to be told his condition, and was informed that
it was so critical he must not be disturbed,
especially by her, who was practically respon-
sible for all his trouble. Then she insisted on
knowing whether he was conscious and whether
he had asked for a priest, and when informed
that Father Foley had already arrived, it re-

quired the strength of four men to hold her. She raved like a maniac, and her screams appalled the garrison. But screams and struggles were all in vain. "Pills the Less" sent for his senior, and "Pills the Pitiless" more than ever deserved his name. He sent for a strait-jacket, saw her securely stowed away in that and borne over to a vacant room in the old hospital, set the steward's wife on watch and a sentry at the door, went back to Waring's bedside, where Sam lay tossing in burning fever, murmured his few words of caution to Pierce and Ferry, then hastened back to where poor Doyle was gasping in agony of mind and body, clinging to the hand of the gentle soldier of the cross, gazing piteously into his father confessor's eyes, drinking in his words of exhortation, yet unable to make articulate reply. The flames had done their cruel work. Only in desperate pain could he speak again.

It was nearly dark when Mrs. Cram came driving back to barracks, bringing Mr. Reynolds with her. Her eyes were dilated, her cheeks flushed with excitement, as she sprang from the low phaeton, and, with a murmured "Come to me as soon as you can" to her hus-

band, she sped away up the stairs, leaving him
to receive and entertain her passenger.

"I, too, went to see Madame Lascelles late
this afternoon," said Reynolds. "I wished to
show her this."

It was a copy of a despatch to the chief of
police of New Orleans. It stated in effect that
Philippe Lascelles had not been seen or heard
of around Key West for over two weeks. It
was believed that he had gone to Havana.

"Can you get word of this to our friend the
detective?" asked Cram.

"I have wired already. He has gone to
Georgia. What I hoped to do was to note the
effect of this on Madame Lascelles; but she was
too ill to see me. Luckily, Mrs. Cram was there,
and I sent it up to her. She will tell you. Now
I have to see Braxton."

And then came a messenger to ask Cram to
join the doctor at Doyle's quarters at once: so
he scurried up-stairs to see Nell first and learn
her tidings.

"Did I not tell you?" she exclaimed, as he
entered the parlor. "Philippe Lascelles was
here that very night, and had been seen with his
brother at the office on Royal Street twice before

this thing happened, and they had trouble about
money. Oh, I made her understand. I appealed to her as a woman to do what she could
to right Mr. Waring, who was so generally believed to be the guilty man. I told her we had
detectives tracing Philippe and would soon find
how and when he reached New Orleans. Finally
I showed her the despatch that Mr. Reynolds
sent up, and at last she broke down, burst into
tears, and said she, too, had learned since the
inquest that Philippe was with her husband, and
probably was the stranger referred to, that awful
night. She even suspected it at the time, for
she knew he came not to borrow but to demand
money that was rightfully his, and also certain
papers that Armand held and that now were
gone. It was she who told me of Philippe's
having been seen with Armand at the office, but
she declared she could not believe that he would
kill her husband. I pointed out the fact that
Armand had fired two shots from his pistol,
apparently, and that no bullet-marks had been
found in the room where the quarrel took place,
and that if his shots had taken effect on his
antagonist he simply could not have been Waring, for though Waring had been bruised and

beaten about the head, the doctor said there was
no sign of bullet-mark about him anywhere.
She recognized the truth of this, but still she
said she believed that there was a quarrel or was
to be a quarrel between her husband and Mr.
Waring. Otherwise I believe her throughout.
I believe that, no matter what romance there
was about her nursing Philippe and his falling
in love with her, she did not encourage him, did
not call him here again, was true to her old
husband. She is simply possessed with the idea
that the quarrel which killed her husband was
between himself and Mr. Waring, and that it
occurred after Philippe had got his money and
papers, and gone."

"W-e-e-ll, Philippe will have a heap to explain when he is found," was Cram's reply.
"Now I have to go to Doyle's. He is making
some confession, I expect, to the priest."

But Cram never dreamed for an instant what
that was to be.

That night poor Doyle's spirit took its flight,
and the story of misery he had to tell, partly
by scrawling with a pencil, partly by gesture
in reply to question, partly in painfully-gasped
sentences, a few words at a time, was practically

this. Lascelles and his party did indeed leave him at the Pelican when he was so drunk he only vaguely knew what was going on or what had happened in the bar-room where they were drinking, but his wife had told him the whole story. Lascelles wanted more drink,—champagne; the bar-tender wanted to close up. They bought several bottles, however, and had them put in the cab, and Lascelles was gay and singing, and, instead of going directly home, insisted on stopping to make a call on the lady who occupied the upper floor of the house Doyle rented on the levee. Doyle rarely saw her, but she sometimes wrote to Lascelles and got Bridget to take the letters to him. She was setting her cap for the old Frenchman. "We called her Mrs. Dawson." The cabman drove very slowly through the storm as Doyle walked home along with Bridget and some man who was helping, and when they reached the gate there was the cab and Waring in it. The cab-driver was standing by his horse, swearing at the delay and saying he would charge double fare. Doyle had had trouble with his wife for many years, and renewed trouble lately because of two visits Lascelles had paid there, and that evening when she sent for him he was drinking in Waring's room, had been drinking during the day; he dreaded more trouble, and 'twas he who took Waring's knife, and still had it, he said, when he entered the gate, and no sooner did he see Lascelles at his door than he ordered him to leave. Lascelles refused to go. Doyle knocked him down, and the Frenchman sprang up, swearing vengeance. Lascelles fired two shots, and Doyle struck once, —with the knife,—and there lay Lascelles, dead, before Doyle could know or realize what he was doing. In fact, Doyle never did know. It was what his wife had told him, and life had been a hell to him ever since that woman came back. She had blackmailed him, more or less, ever since he got his commission, because of an old trouble he'd had in Texas.

And this confession was written out for him, signed by Doyle on his dying bed, duly witnessed, and the civil authorities were promptly notified. Bridget Doyle was handed over to the police. Certain detectives out somewhere on the trail of somebody else were telegraphed to come in, and four days later, when the force of the fever was broken and Waring lay weak, languid, but returning to his senses, Cram and the doctor read the confession to their patient, and then started to their feet as he almost sprang from the bed.

"It's an infernal lie!" he weakly cried. "I took that knife from Doyle and kept it. I myself saw Lascelles to his gate, safe and sound."

Florence E. Johnson

CHAPTER XI.

THE sunshine of an exquisite April morning
was shimmering over the Louisiana lowlands as
Battery "X" was "hitching in," and Mrs. Cram's
pretty pony-phaeton came flashing through the
garrison gate and reined up in front of the guns.
A proud and happy woman was Mrs. Cram, and
daintily she gathered the spotless, cream-colored
reins and slanted her long English driving-whip
at the exact angle prescribed by the vogue of the
day. By her side, reclining luxuriously on his
pillows, was Sam Waring, now senior first lieutenant of the battery, taking his first airing since
his strange illness. Pallid and thin though he
was, that young gentleman was evidently capable
of appreciating to the fullest extent the devoted
attentions of which he had been the object ever
since his return. Stanch friend and fervent
champion of her husband's most distinguished
officer at any time, Mrs. Cram had thrown herself into his cause with a zeal that challenged

the admiration even of the men whom she mercilessly snubbed because they had accepted the general verdict that Lascelles had died by Waring's hand. Had they met in the duello as practised in the South in those days, sword to sword, or armed with pistol at twelve paces, she would have shuddered, but maintained that as a soldier and gentleman Waring could not have refused his opponent's challenge, inexcusable though such challenge might have been. But that he could have stooped to vulgar, unregulated fracas, without seconds or the formality of the cartel, first with fists and those women's weapons, nails, then knives or stilettoes, as though he was some low dago or Sicilian,—why, that was simply and utterly incredible. None the less she was relieved and rejoiced, as were all Waring's friends, when the full purport of poor Doyle's dying confession was noised abroad. Even those who were sceptical were now silenced. For four days her comfort and relief had been inexpressible; and then came the hour when, with woe and trouble in his face, her husband returned to her from Waring's bedside with the incomprehensible tidings that he had utterly repudiated Doyle's confession,—had, in-

deed, said that which could probably only serve
to renew the suspicion of his own guilt, or else
justify the theory that he was demented.

Though Cram and the doctor warned Waring not to talk, talk he would, to Pierce, to
Ferry, to Ananias; and though these three
were pledged by Cram to reveal to no one what
Waring said, it plunged them in an agony of
doubt and misgiving. Day after day had the
patient told and re-told the story, and never
could cross-questioning shake him in the least.
Cram sent for Reynolds and took him into their
confidence, and Reynolds heard the story and
added his questions, but to no effect. From
first to last he remembered every incident up to
his parting with Lascelles at his own gateway.
After that—nothing.

His story, in brief, was as follows. He was
both surprised and concerned, while smoking
and chatting with Mr. Allerton in the rotunda
of the St. Charles, to see Lascelles with a friend,
evidently watching an opportunity of speaking
with him. He had noticed about a week previous a marked difference in the old Frenchman's manner, and three days before the tragedy, when calling on his way from town to see

Madame and Nin Nin, was informed that they were not at home, and Monsieur himself was the informant; nor did he, as heretofore, invite Waring to enter. Sam was a fellow who detested misunderstanding. Courteously, but positively, he demanded explanation. Lascelles shrugged his shoulders, but gave it. He had heard too much of Monsieur's attentions to Madame his wife, and desired their immediate discontinuance. He must request Monsieur's assurance that he would not again visit Beau Rivage, or else the reparation due a man of honor, etc. "Whereupon," said Waring, "I didn't propose to be outdone in civility, and therefore replied, in the best French I could command, 'Permit me to tender Monsieur—both. Monsieur's friends will find me at the barracks.'"

"All the same," said Waring, "when I found Madame and Nin Nin stuck in the mud I did what I considered the proper thing, and drove them, *coram publico*, to 'bonne maman's,' never letting them see, of course, that there was any row on tap, and so when I saw the old fellow with a keen-looking party alongside I felt sure it meant mischief. I was utterly surprised, there-

fore, when Lascelles came up with hat off and
hand extended, bowing low, praying pardon for
the intrusion, but saying he could not defer
another instant the desire to express his gratitude the most profound for my extreme courtesy
to Madame and his beloved child. He had
heard the whole story, and, to my confusion,
insisted on going over all the details before
Allerton, even to my heroism, as he called it, in
knocking down that big bully of a cabman. I
was confused, yet couldn't shake him off. He
was persistent. He was abject. He begged to
meet my friend, to present his, to open champagne and drink eternal friendship. He would
change the name of his *château*—the rotten old
rookery—from Beau Rivage to Belle Alliance.
He would make this day a *fête* in the calendar
of the Lascelles family. And then it began to
dawn on me that he had been drinking champagne before he came. I did not catch the
name of the other gentleman, a much younger
man. He was very ceremonious and polite, but
distant. Then, in some way, came up the fact
that I had been trying to get a cab to take me
back to barracks, and then Lascelles declared
that nothing could be more opportune. He had

secured a carriage and was just going down with
Monsieur. They had *des affaires* to transact at
once. He took me aside and said, 'In proof
that you accept my *amende*, and in order that I
may make to you my personal apologies, you
must accept my invitation.' So go with them I
did. I was all the time thinking of Cram's mys-
terious note bidding me return at taps. I couldn't
imagine what was up, but I made my best en-
deavors to get a cab. None was to be had, so I
was really thankful for this opportunity. All the
way down Lascelles overwhelmed me with civili-
ties, and I could only murmur and protest, and
the other party only murmured approbation.
He hardly spoke English at all. Then Lascelles
insisted on a stop at the Pelican and on bumpers
of champagne, and there, as luck would have
it, was Doyle,—drunk, as usual, and determined
to join the party; and though I endeavored to
put him aside, Lascelles would not have it. He
insisted on being presented to the comrade of
his gallant friend, and in the private room where
we went he overwhelmed Doyle with details of
our grand reconciliation and with bumper after
bumper of Krug. This enabled me to fight
shy of the wine, but in ten minutes Doyle was

fighting drunk, Lascelles tipsy. The driver
came in for his pay, saying he would go no
further. They had a row. Lascelles wouldn't
pay; called him an Irish thief, and all that. I
slipped my last V into the driver's hand and
got him out somehow. Monsieur Philippes, or
whatever his name was, said he would go out,—
he'd get a cab in the neighborhood; and the
next thing I knew, Lascelles and Doyle were in
a fury of a row. Lascelles said all the Irish
were knaves and blackguards and swindlers, and
Doyle stumbled around after him. Out came a
pistol! Out came a knife! I tripped Doyle
and got him into a chair, and was so intent on
pacifying him and telling him not to make a
fool of himself that I didn't notice anything else.
I handled him good-naturedly, got the knife
away, and then was amazed to find that he had
my own pet paper-cutter. I made them shake
hands and make up. It was all a mistake, said
Lascelles. But what made it a worse mistake,
the old man *would* order more wine, and, with it,
brandy. He insisted on celebrating this second
grand reconciliation, and then both got drunker,
but the tall Frenchman had Lascelles's pistol
and I had the knife, and then a cab came, and,

though it was storming beastly and I had Ferry's duds on and Larkin's best tile and Pierce's umbrella, we bundled in somehow and drove on down the levee, leaving Doyle in the hands of that Amazon of a wife of his and a couple of doughboys who happened to be around there. Now Lascelles was all hilarity, singing, joking, confidential. Nothing would do but we must stop and call on a lovely woman, a *belle amie.* He could rely on our discretion, he said, laying his finger on his nose, and looking sly and coquettish, for all the world like some old *roué* of a Frenchman. He must stop and see her and take her some wine. 'Indeed,' he said, mysteriously, 'it is a rendezvous.' Well, I was their guest; I had no money. What could I do? It was then after eleven, I should judge. Monsieur Philippes, or whatever his name was, gave orders to the driver. We pulled up, and then, to my surprise, I found we were at Doyle's. That ended it. I told them they must excuse me. They protested, but of course I couldn't go in there. So they took a couple of bottles apiece and went in the gate, and I settled myself for a nap and got it. I don't know how long I slept, but I was aroused by the devil's own tumult.

A shot had been fired. Men and women both
were screaming and swearing. Some one suddenly burst into the cab beside me, really
pushed from behind, and then away we went
through the mud and the rain; and the lightning was flashing now, and presently I could
recognize Lascelles, raging. 'Infâme!' 'Co-
quin!' 'Assassin!' were the mildest terms he
was volleying at somebody; and then, recogniz-
ing me, he burst into maudlin tears, swore I was
his only friend. He had been insulted, abused,
denied reparation. Was he hurt? I inquired,
and instinctively felt for my knife. It was still
there where I'd hid it in the inside pocket of
my overcoat. No hurt; not a blow. Did I suppose that he, a Frenchman, would pardon that
or leave the spot until satisfaction had been
exacted? Then I begged him to be calm and
listen to me for a moment. I told him my
plight,—that I had given my word to be at
barracks that evening; that I had no money left,
but I could go no further. Instantly he forgot
his woes and became absorbed in my affairs.
'*Parole d'honneur!*' he would see that mine was
never unsullied. He himself would escort me
to the *maison de* Capitaine Cram. He would re-

joice to say to that brave ennemi, Behold! here is thy lieutenant, of honor the most unsullied, of courage the most admirable, of heart the most magnanimous. The Lord only knows what he wouldn't have done had we not pulled up at his gate. There I helped him out on the banquette. He was steadied by his row, whatever it had been. He would not let me expose myself — even under Pierce's umbrella. He would not permit me to suffer 'from times so of the dog.' 'You will drive Monsieur to his home and return here for me at once,' he ordered cabby, grasped both my hands with fervent good-night and the explanation that he had much haste, implored pardon for leaving me,— on the morrow he would call and explain everything,—then darted into the gate. We never could have parted on more friendly terms. I stood a moment to see that he safely reached his door, for a light was dimly burning in the hall, then turned to jump into the cab, but it wasn't there. Nothing was there. I jumped from the banquette into a berth aboard some steamer out at sea. They tell me the first thing I asked for was Pierce's umbrella and Larkin's hat."

And this was the story that Waring maintained from first to last. "Pills" ventured a query as to whether the amount of Krug and Clicquot consumed might not have overthrown his mental equipoise. No, Sam declared, he drank very little. "The only bacchanalian thing I did was to join in a jovial chorus from a new French opera which Lascelles's friend piped up and I had heard in the North:

> .Oui, buvons, buvons encore !
> S'il est un vin qu'on adore
> De Paris à Macao,
> C'est le Clicquot, c'est le Clicquot."

Asked if he had formed any conjecture as to the identity of the stranger, Sam said no. The name sounded like "Philippes," but he couldn't be sure. But when told that there were rumors to the effect that Lascelles's younger brother had been seen with him twice or thrice of late, and that he had been in exile because, if anything, of a hopeless passion for Madame his sister-in-law, and that his name was Philippe, Waring looked dazed. Then a sudden light, as of newer, fresher memory, flashed up in his eyes. He seemed about to speak, but as suddenly controlled himself and turned his face to the wall. From that time on he was determinedly dumb about the stranger. What roused him to lively interest and conjecture, however, was Cram's query as to whether he had not recognized in the cabman, called in by the stranger, the very one whom he had "knocked endwise" and who had tried to shoot him that morning. "No," said Waring: "the man did not speak at all, that I noticed, and I did not once see his face, he was so bundled up against the storm." But if it was the same party, suggested he, it seemed hardly necessary to look any further in explanation of his own disappearance. Cabby had simply squared matters by knocking him senseless, helping himself to his watch and ring, and turning out his pockets, then hammering him until frightened off, and then, to cover his tracks, setting him afloat in Anatole's boat.

"Perhaps cabby took a hand in the murder, too," suggested Sam, with eager interest. "You say he had disappeared,—gone with his plunder. Now, who else could have taken my knife?"

Then Reynolds had something to tell him: that the "lady" who wrote the anonymous letters, the *belle amie* whom Lascelles proposed to

18

visit, the occupant of the upper floor of "the dove-cot," was none other than the blighted floweret who had appealed to him for aid and sympathy, for fifty dollars at first and later for more, the first year of his army service in the South, "for the sake of the old home." Then Waring grew even more excited and interested. "Pills" put a stop to further developments for a few days. He feared a relapse. But, in spite of "Pills," the developments, like other maladies, throve. The little detective came down again. He was oddly inquisitive about that *chanson à boire* from "*Fleur de Thé.*" Would Mr. Waring hum it for him? And Sam, now sitting up in his parlor, turned to his piano, and with long, slender, fragile-looking fingers rattled a lively prelude and then faintly quavered the rollicking words.

"Odd," said Mr. Pepper, as they had grown to call him, "I heard that sung by a fellow up in Chartres Street two nights hand-running before this thing happened,—a merry cuss, too, with a rather loose hand on his shekels. Lots of people may know it, though, mayn't they?"

"No, indeed, not down here," said Sam. "It only came out in New York within the last

four months, and hasn't been South or West at
all, that I know of. What did he look like?"

"Well, what did the feller that was with you
look like?"   J

But here Sam's description grew vague. So
Pepper went up to have a beer by himself at
the *café chantant* on Chartres Street, and didn't
return for nearly a week.

Meantime came this exquisite April morning
and Sam's appearance in the pony-phaeton in
front of Battery "X." Even the horses seemed
to prick up their ears and be glad to see him.
Grim old war sergeants rode up to touch their
caps and express the hope that they'd soon have
the lieutenant in command of the right section
again,—"not but what Loot'n't Ferry's doing
first-rate, sir,"—and for a few minutes, as his fair
charioteer drove him around the battery, in his
weak, languid voice, Waring indulged in a little
of his own characteristic chaffing:

"I expect you to bring this section up to top
notch, Mr. Ferry, as I am constitutionally op-
posed to any work on my own account. I beg to
call your attention, sir, to the fact that it's very
bad form to appear with full-dress *schabraque* on
your horse when the battery is in fatigue. The

red blanket, sir, the red blanket only should be used. Be good enough to stretch your traces there, right caisson. Yes, I thought so, swing trace is twisted. Carelessness, Mr. Ferry, and indifference to duty are things I won't tolerate. Your cheek-strap, too, sir, is an inch too long. Your bit will fall through that horse's mouth. This won't do, sir, not in my section, sir. I'll fine you a box of Partagas if it occurs again."

But the blare of the bugle sounding "attention" announced the presence of the battery commander. Nell whipped up in an instant and whisked her invalid out of the way.

"Good-morning, Captain Cram," said he, as he passed his smiling chief. "I regret to observe, sir, that things have been allowed to run down somewhat in my absence."

"Oh, out with you, you combination of cheek and incapacity, or I'll run you down with the whole battery. Oh! Waring, some gentlemen in a carriage have just stopped at your quarters, all in black, too. Ah, here's the orderly now."

And the card, black-bordered, handed into the phaeton, bore a name which blanched Waring's face :

"Why, what is it, Waring?" asked Cram, anxiously, bending down from his saddle.

For a moment Waring was silent. Mrs. Cram felt her own hand trembling.

"Can you turn the battery over to Ferry and come with me?" asked the lieutenant.

"Certainly.—Bugler, report to Lieutenant Ferry and tell him I shall have to be absent for a while.—Drive on, Nell."

When, five minutes later, Waring was assisted up the stair-way, Cram towering on his right, the little party came upon a group of strangers, —three gentlemen, one of whom stepped courteously forward, raising his hat in a black-gloved hand. He was of medium height, slender, erect, and soldierly in bearing; his face was dark and oval, his eyes large, deep, and full of light. He

o   18*

spoke mainly in English, but with marked accent, and the voice was soft and melodious:

"I fear I have intrude. Have I the honor to address Lieutenant Waring? I am Philippe Lascelles."

For a moment Waring was too amazed to speak. At last, with brightening face and hold ing forth his hand, he said,—

"I am most glad to meet you,—to know that it was not you who drove down with us that night."

"Alas, no! I left Armand but that very morning, returning to Havana, thence going to Santiago. It was not until five days ago the news reached me. It is of that stranger I come to ask."

It was an odd council gathered there in Waring's room in the old barracks that April morning while Ferry was drilling the battery to his heart's content and the infantry companies were wearily going over the manual or bayonet exercise. Old Brax had been sent for, and came. Monsieur Lascelles's friends, both, like himself, soldiers of the South, were presented, and for their information Waring's story was again told, with only most delicate allusion to certain incidents which might be considered as reflecting on the character and dignity of the elder brother. And then Philippe told his. True, there had been certain transactions between Armand and himself. He had fully trusted his brother, a man of affairs, with the management of the little inheritance which he, a soldier, had no idea how to handle, and Armand's business had suffered greatly by the war. It was touching to see how in every word the younger strove to conceal the fact that the elder had misapplied the securities and had been practically faithless to his trust. Everything, he declared, had been finally settled as between them that very morning before his return to Havana. Armand had brought to him early all papers remaining in his possession and had paid him what was justly due. He knew, however, that Armand was now greatly embarrassed in his affairs. They had parted with fond embrace, the most affectionate of brothers. But Philippe had been seeing and hearing enough to make him gravely apprehensive as to Armand's future, to know that his business was rapidly going down-hill, that he had been raising money in various ways, speculating, and had fallen into the hands of sharpers, and yet

Armand would not admit it, would not consent
to accept help or to use his younger brother's
property in any way. "The lawyer," said
Philippe, "informed me that Beau Rivage was
heavily mortgaged, and it is feared that there
will be nothing left for Madame and Nin Nin,
though, for that matter, they shall never want."
What he had also urged, and he spoke with
reluctance here, and owned it only because the
detectives told him it was now well known, was
that Armand had of late been playing the *rôle*
of *galant homme*, and that the woman in the case
had fled. Of all this he felt, he said, bound to
speak fully, because in coming here with his
witnesses to meet Lieutenant Waring and his
friends he had two objects in view. The first
was to admit that he had accepted as fact the
published reports that Lieutenant Waring was
probably his brother's slayer; had hastened back
to New Orleans to demand justice or obtain revenge; had here learned from the lawyers and
police that there were now other and much more
probable theories, having heard only one of
which he had cried "Enough," and had come to
pray the forgiveness of Mr. Waring for having
believed an officer and a gentleman guilty of so

foul a crime. Second, he had come to invoke his aid in running down the murderer. Philippe was affected almost to tears.

"There is one question I must beg to ask Monsieur," said Waring, as the two clasped hands. "Is there not still a member of your family who entertains the idea that it was I who killed Armand Lascelles?"

And Philippe was deeply embarrassed.

"Ah, monsieur," he answered, "I could not venture to intrude myself upon a grief so sacred. I have not seen Madame, and who is there who could—who would—tell her of Armand's——" And Philippe broke off abruptly, with despairing shrug, and outward wave of his slender hand.

"Let us try to see that she never does know," said Waring. "These are the men we need to find: the driver of the cab, the stranger whose name sounded so like yours, a tall, swarthy, black-haired, black-eyed fellow with pointed moustache——"

"*C'est lui! c'est bien lui!*" exclaimed Lascelles, —"the very man who insisted on entering the private office where, Armand and I, we close our affairs that morning. His whispered words make my brother all of pale, and yet he go off humming to himself."

"Oh, we'll nail him," said Cram. "Two of the best detectives in the South are on his trail now."

And then came Ananias with a silver tray, champagne, and glasses (from Mrs. Cram), and the conference went on another hour before the guests went off.

"Bless my soul!" said Brax, whose diameter seemed in no wise increased by the quart of Roederer he had swallowed with such gusto,— "bless my soul! and to think I believed that we were going to have a duel with some of those fellows a fortnight or so ago!"

Then entered "Pills" and ordered Waring back to bed. He was sleeping placidly when, late that evening, Reynolds and Cram came tearing up the stair-way, full of great news; but the doctor said not to wake him.

Meantime, how fared it with that bruised reed, the lone widow of the late Lieutenant Doyle? Poor old Jim had been laid away with military honors under the flag at Chalmette, and his faithful Bridget was spending the days in the public calaboose. Drunk and disorderly was the charge on which she had been arraigned, and, though she declared herself abundantly able to pay her fine twice over, Mr. Pepper had warned the authorities to keep her under lock and key and out of liquor, as her testimony would be of vital importance, if for nothing better than to send her up for perjury. Now she was alternately wheedling, cursing, coaxing, bribing; all to no purpose. The agent of the Lemaître property had swooped down on the dove-cot and found a beggarly array of empty bottles and a good deal of discarded feminine gear scattered about on both floors. One room in which certain detectives were vastly interested contained the unsavory relics of a late supper. Three or four empty champagne-bottles, some shattered glasses, and, what seemed most to attract them, various stubs of partially-consumed cigarettes, lay about the tables and floor. Adjoining this was the chamber which had been known as Mrs. Dawson's, and this, too, had been thoroughly explored. 'Loucette, who had disappeared after Doyle's tragic death, was found not far away, and the police thought it but fair that Mrs. Doyle should not be deprived of the services of her maid. Then came other additions, though

confined in other sections of the city.   Mr.
Pepper wired that the party known as Monsieur Philippes had been run to earth and would
reach town with him by train about the same
time that another of the force returned from Mo-
bile by boat, bringing a young man known as
Dawson and wanted as a deserter, and a very
sprightly young lady who appeared to move in a
higher sphere of life, but was unquestionably his
wife, for the officer could prove their marriage
in South Carolina in the spring of '65.   As Mr.
Pepper expressed it when he reported to Reynolds, "It's almost a full hand, but, for a fact,
it's only a bobtail flush.   We need that cabman
to fill."

"How did you trace Philippes?" asked Reynolds.

"Him?   Oh, he was too darned musical.   It
was—what do you call it?—Flure de Tay that
did for him.   Why, he's the fellow that raised
all the money and most of the h—ll for this old
man Lascelles.   He'd been sharping him for
years."

"Well, when can we bring this thing to a
head?" asked the aide-de-camp.

"*Poco tiempo!* by Saturday, I reckon."

But it came sooner.

Waring was seated one lovely evening in a low reclining chair on Mrs. Cram's broad gallery, sipping contentedly at the cup of fragrant tea she had handed him. The band was playing, and a number of children were chasing about in noisy glee. The men were at supper, the officers, as a rule, at mess. For several minutes the semi-restored invalid had not spoken a word. In one of his customary day-dreams he had been calmly gazing at the shapely white hand of his hostess, "all queenly with its weight of rings."

"Will you permit me to examine those rings a moment?" he said.

"Why, certainly. No, you sit still, Mr. Waring," she replied, promptly rising, and, pulling them off her fingers, dropped them into his open palm. With the same dreamy expression on his clear-cut, pallid face, he turned them over and over, held them up to the light, finally selected one exquisite gem, and then, half rising, held forth the others. As she took them and still stood beside his chair as though patiently waiting, he glanced up.

"Oh, beg pardon. You want this, I suppose?"

and, handing her the dainty teacup, he calmly slipped the ring into his waistcoat-pocket and languidly murmured, "Thanks."

"Well, I like that."

"Yes? So do I, rather better than the others."

"May I ask what you purpose doing with my ring?"

"I was just thinking. I've ordered a new Amidon for Larkin, a new ninety-dollar suit for Ferry, and I shall be decidedly poor this month, even if we recover Merton's watch."

"Oh, well, if it's only to pawn one, why not take a diamond?"

"But it isn't."

"What then, pray?"

"Well, again I was just thinking—whether I could find another to match this up in town, or send this one—to her."

"Mr. *Waring! Really?*" And now Mrs. Cram's bright eyes are dancing with eagerness and delight.

For all answer, though his own eyes begin to moisten and swim, he draws from an inner pocket a dainty letter, post-marked from a far, far city to the northeast.

" You *dear* fellow! IIow can I tell you how
glad I am! I haven't dared to ask you of her
since we met at Washington, but—oh, my heart
has been just full of her since—since this trouble
came."

" God bless the trouble! it was that that won
her to me at last. I have loved her ever since
I first saw her—long years ago."

"Oh! *oh!* oh! if Ned were only here! I'm
wild to tell him. I may, mayn't I?"

" Yes, the moment he comes."

But Ned brought a crowd with him when he
got back from town a little later. Reynolds
was there, and Philippe Lascelles, and Mr. Pepper, and they had a tale to tell that must needs
be condensed.

They had all been present by invitation of the
civil authorities at a very dramatic affair during
the late afternoon,—the final lifting of the veil
that hid from public view the " strange, eventful
history" of the Lascelles tragedy. Cram was
the spokesman by common consent. "With
the exception of the Dawsons," said he, " none
of the parties implicated knew up to the hour
of his or her examination that any one of the
others was to appear." Mrs. Dawson, eager to

save her own pretty neck, had told her story
without reservation.   Dawson knew nothing.

The story had been wrung from her piece-
meal, but was finally told in full, and in the
presence of the officers and civilians indicated.
She had married in April, '65, to the scorn of
her people, a young Yankee officer attached to
the commissary department. She had starved all
through the war. She longed for life, luxury,
comforts. She had nothing but her beauty, he
nothing but his pay.   The extravagances of a
month swamped him; the drink and desperation
of the next ruined him.   He maintained her in
luxury at the best hotel only a few weeks, then
all of his and much of Uncle Sam's money was
gone.   Inspection proved him a thief and em-
bezzler.   He fled, and she was abandoned to her
own resources.   She had none but her beauty
and a gift of penmanship which covered the
many sins of her orthography.   She was given
a clerkship, but wanted more money, and took
it, blackmailing a quartermaster.   She imposed
on Waring, but he quickly found her out and
absolutely refused afterwards to see her at all.
She was piqued and angered, "a woman scorned,"
but not until he joined Battery "X" did oppor-

tunity present itself for revenge. She had
secured a room under Mrs. Doyle's reputable
roof, to be near the barracks, where she could
support herself by writing for Mrs. Doyle and
blackmailing those whom she lured, and where
she could watch *him*, and, to her eager delight,
she noted and prepared to make much of his
attentions to Madame Lascelles. Incidentally,
too, she might inveigle the susceptible Lascelles
himself, on the principle that there's no fool like
an old fool. Mrs. Doyle lent herself eagerly to
the scheme. The letters began to pass to and
fro again. Lascelles was fool enough to answer,
and when, all on a sudden, Mrs. Doyle's "long-
missing relative," as she called him, turned up,
a pensioner on her charity, it was through the
united efforts of the two women he got a situation as cab-driver at the stable up at the east-
ern skirt of the town. Dawson had enlisted to
keep from starving, and, though she had no use
for him as a husband, he would do to fetch and
carry, and he dare not disobey. Twice when
Doyle was battery officer of the day did this
strangely-assorted pair of women entertain Lascelles at supper and fleece him out of what
money he had. Then came Philippes with Las-

celles in Mike's cab, as luck would have it, but they could not fleece Philippes. Old Lascelles was rapidly succumbing to Nita's fascinations when came the night of the terrible storm. Mike had got to drinking, and was laid low by the lieutenant. Mike and Bridget both vowed vengeance. But meantime Doyle himself had got wind of something that was going on, and he and his tyrant had a fearful row. He commanded her never to allow a man inside the premises when he was away, and, though brought home drunk that awful night, furiously ordered the Frenchman out, and might have assaulted them had not Bridget lassoed him with a chloroformed towel. That was the last he knew until another day. Lascelles, Philippes, and she, Mrs. Dawson, had already drunk a bottle of champagne when interrupted by Doyle's coming. Lascelles was tipsy, had snatched his pistol and fired a shot to frighten Doyle, but had only enraged him, and then he had to run for his cab. He was bundled in and Doyle disposed of. It was only three blocks down to Beau Rivage, and thither Mike drove them in all the storm. She did not know at the time of Waring's being in the cab. In less than fifteen

minutes Mike was back and called excitedly for
Bridget; had a hurried consultation with her;
she seized a waterproof and ran out with him,
but darted back and took the bottle of chloroform she had used on her husband, now lying
limp and senseless on a sofa below, and then she
disappeared. When half an hour passed and
Lascelles failed to return with them, bringing
certain papers of which he'd been speaking to
Philippes, the latter declared there must be
something wrong, and went out to reconnoitre
despite the storm. He could see nothing. It
was after midnight when Mrs. Doyle came rushing in, gasping, all out of breath "along of
the storm," she said. She had been down the
levee with Mike to find a cushion and lap-robe
he dropped and couldn't afford to lose. They
never could have found it at all "but for ould
Lascelles lending them a lantern." He wanted
Mike to bring down two bottles of champagne
he'd left here, but it was storming so that he
would not venture again, and Lieutenant Waring, she said, was going to spend the night
with Lascelles at Beau Rivage: Mike couldn't
drive any further down towards the barracks.
Lascelles sent word to Philippes that he'd bring

up the papers first thing in the morning, if the storm lulled, and Philippes went out indignant at all the time lost, but Mike swore he'd not drive down again for a fortune. So the Frenchman got into the cab and went up with him to town. The moment he was gone Mrs. Doyle declared she was dead tired, used up, and drank huge goblets of the wine until she reeled off to her room, leaving an apron behind. Then Mrs. Dawson went to her own room, after putting out the lights, and when, two days later, she heard the awful news of the murder, knowing that investigation would follow and she and her sins be brought to light, she fled, for she had enough of his money in her possession, and poor demented Dawson, finding her gone, followed.

Philippes's story corroborated this in every particular. The last he saw of the cab or of the cabman was near the house of the hook-and-ladder company east of the French Market. The driver there said his horse was dead beat and could do no more, so Philippes went into the market, succeeded in getting another cab by paying a big price, slept at Cassidy's, waited all the morning about Lascelles's place, and finally, having to return to the Northeast at once, he took the evening train on the Jackson road and never heard of the murder until ten days after. He was amazed at his arrest.

And then came before his examiners a mere physical wreck,—the shadow of his former self, —caught at the high tide of a career of crime and debauchery, a much less bulky party than the truculent Jehu of Madame Lascelles's cab, yet no less important a witness than that same driver. He was accompanied by a priest. He had been brought hither in an ambulance from the Hôtel-Dieu, where he had been traced several days before and found almost at death's door. His confession was most important of all. He had struck Lieutenant Waring as that officer turned away from Lascelles's gate, intending only to down and then kick and hammer him, but he had struck with a lead-loaded rubber club, and he was horrified to see him drop like one dead. Then he lost his nerve and drove furiously back for Bridget. Together they returned, and found Waring lying there as he had left him on the dripping banquette. "You've killed him, Mike. There's only one thing to do," she said: "take his watch and everything valuable he has, and we'll throw him over on the levee." She herself

P

took the knife from his overcoat-pocket, lest
he should recover suddenly, and then, said the
driver, "even as we were bending over him
there came a sudden flash of lightning, and
there was Lascelles bending over us, demanding
to know what it meant. Then like another flash
he seemed to realize what was up, sprang back,
and drew pistol. He had caught us in the act.
There was nothing else to do; we both sprang
upon him. He fired, and hit me, but only in
the arm, and before he could pull trigger again
we both grappled him. I seized his gun, Bridget
his throat, but he screamed and fought like a
tiger, then wilted all of a sudden. I was scared
and helpless, but she had her wits about her,
and told me what to do. The lieutenant began
to gasp and revive just then, so she soaked the
handkerchief in chloroform and placed it over
his mouth, and together we lifted him into the
cab. Then we raised Lascelles and carried him
in and laid him on his sofa, for he had left the
door open and the lamp on the table. Bridget
had been there before, and knew all about the
house. We set the pistol back in his hand, but
couldn't make the fingers grasp it. We ran-
sacked the desk and got what money there was,

locked and bolted the doors, and climbed out of the side window, under which she dropped the knife among the bushes. 'They'll never suspect us in the world, Mike,' she said. 'It's the lieutenant's knife that did it, and, as he was going to fight him anyhow, he'll get the credit of it all.' Then we drove up the levee, put Waring in Anatole's boat, sculls and all, and shoved him off. 'I'll muzzle Jim,' she said. 'I'll make him believe 'twas he that did it when he was drunk.' She took most of the money, and the watch and ring. She said she could hide them until they'd be needed. Then I drove Philippes up to town until I began to get so sick and faint I could do no more. I turned the cab loose and got away to a house where I knew they'd take care of me, and from there, when my money was gone, they sent me to the hospital, thinking I was dying. I swear to God I never meant to more than get square with the lieutenant. I never struck Lascelles at all; 'twas she who drove the knife into his heart."

Then, exhausted, he was led into an adjoining room, and Mrs. Doyle was marched in, the picture of injured Irish innocence. For ten minutes, with wonderful effrontery and nerve, she denied all personal participation in the crime, and faced her inquisitors with brazen calm. Then the chief quietly turned and signalled. An officer led forward from one side the wreck of a cabman, supported by the priest; a door opened on the other, and, escorted by another policeman, Mrs. Dawson re-entered, holding in her hands outstretched a gingham apron on which were two deep stains the shape and size of a long, straight-bladed, two-edged knife. It was the apron that Bridget Doyle had worn that fatal night. One quick, furtive look at that, one glance at her trembling, shrinking, cowering kinsman, and, with an Irish howl of despair, a loud wail of "Mike, Mike, you've sworn your sister's life away!" she threw herself upon the floor, tearing madly at her hair. And so ended the mystery of Beau Rivage.

There was silence a moment in Cram's pretty parlor when the captain had finished his story. Waring was the first to speak:

"There is one point I wish they'd clear up."

"What's that?" said Cram.

"Who's got Merton's watch?"

"Oh, by Jove! I quite forgot. It's all right, Waring. Anatole's place was 'pulled' last night, and he had her valuables all done up in a box. ' To pay for his boat,' he said."

*   *   *   *   *   *

A quarter of a century has passed away since the scarlet plumes of Light Battery " X" were last seen dancing along the levee below New Orleans. Beau Rivage, old and moss-grown at the close of the war, fell into rapid decline after the tragedy of that April night. Heavily mortgaged, the property passed into other hands, but for years never found a tenant. Far and near the negroes spoke of the homestead as haunted, and none of their race could be induced to set foot within its gates. One night the sentry at the guard-house saw sudden light on the westward sky, and then a column of flame. Again the fire-alarm resounded among the echoing walls of the barracks; but when the soldiers reached the scene, a seething ruin was all that was left of the old Southern home. Somebody sent Cram a marked copy of a New Orleans paper, and in their cosey quarters at Fort Hamilton the captain read it aloud to his devoted Nell: " The old house has been vacant, an object of almost superstitious dread to the neighborhood," said the *Times*, " ever since the tragic

20

death of Armand Lascelles in the spring of 1868. In police annals the affair was remarkable because of the extraordinary chain of circumstantial evidence which for a time seemed to fasten the murder upon an officer of the army then stationed at Jackson Barracks, but whose innocence was triumphantly established. Madame Lascelles, it is understood, is now educating her daughter in Paris, whither she removed immediately after her marriage a few months ago to Captain Philippe Lascelles, formerly of the Confederate army, a younger brother of her first husband."

"Well," said Cram, "I'll have to send that to Waring. They're in Vienna by this time, I suppose. Look here, Nell; how was it that when we fellows were fretting about Waring's attentions to Madame, you should have been so serenely superior to it all, even when, as I know, the stories reached you?"

"Ah, Ned, I knew a story worth two of those. He was in love with Natalie Maitland all the time."

THE END.

Mrs. A. L. Wister's Translations.

12mo.   Cloth, $1.00 per volume.

www.ingramcontent.com/pod-product-compliance
Lightning Source LLC
Chambersburg PA
CBHW020115030726
47498CB00006B/2124